DEAD MEN DON'T BLEED

Brothers Ray and Buck Norris quit the Rebel army in 1863 and go their separate ways. Whilst Ray seeks vengeance on those who killed their parents, Buck has had enough of killing, and drifts for eleven years until he reaches Rymansville. There, he immediately runs into trouble. After going to the rescue of a young woman, he is arrested by a marshal who mistakes him for Ray — now a wanted fugitive . . .

WALTER L. BRYANT

DEAD MEN
DON'T BLEED

Complete and Unabridged

LINFORD
Leicester

First published in Great Britain in 2015 by
Robert Hale Limited
London

First Linford Edition
published 2017
by arrangement with
Robert Hale
an imprint of
The Crowood Press
Wiltshire

A catalogue record for this book is available
from the British Library.

ISBN 978–1–4448–3269–3

Published by
F. A. Thorpe (Publishing)
Anstey, Leicestershire

Set by Words & Graphics Ltd.
Anstey, Leicestershire
Printed and bound in Great Britain by
T. J. International Ltd., Padstow, Cornwall

1

Buck Norris gazed down at the collection of buildings which made up the town of Rymansville, less than fifteen minutes' ride away. It looked peaceful. He smiled. Perhaps, after eleven years of drifting, he could find a place here to settle down.

The sound of gunfire broke into his thoughts and he pulled lightly on the reins of the chestnut gelding.

'Whoa,' he murmured. 'Let's see what's happening.' He waited on the crest of the hill with a stand of pines at his back. 'Mebbe some folk're just celebrating,' he muttered.

The gunfire sounded below him and to his right. He identified the occasional crack of a rifle against the more rapid fire of pistols, but whoever was causing the ruckus was hidden behind the trees lining the trail.

'Could be some young bucks letting

1

off steam,' he suggested to his horse. He pulled his Stetson lower and waited, his steel-grey eyes squinting against the glare of the late-afternoon sun. He loosened his bandanna and ran a sleeve over his face to clear away the sweat and dust.

His right hand rested on the stock of the Winchester which had long since replaced the Henry in the saddle boot. He didn't like surprises and, although he had no intention of using the weapon unless he was called upon to do so, he needed to be prepared. He patted the gelding's head.

As he watched, a buggy emerged from the trees, driven fast in the direction of the town. The figure urging the horse to greater speed was holding on to the reins with one hand and the edge of the seat with the other. It wasn't immediately apparent that the driver was a woman, dressed as she was in jeans and loose jacket, but then, as her hat slipped from her head, Buck saw her long flaxen hair flow out behind her.

Then he saw the reason for her haste. Two men on horseback were in pursuit, whooping loudly, shooting as they went. Without further thought Buck urged the gelding forward, aiming for a point where his path would cross with those on the trail.

He reached the trail ahead of the buggy. As he waited for it to pass he noticed that the men behind were firing high as if their intention was to make a noise rather than kill. He drew his .45 and came out from the shelter of the trees, firing warning shots into the air.

The two men were young and clearly didn't take kindly to the interruption. They reined in hard, turning their guns towards him and firing as they came. This time their aim was more accurate.

Buck slipped swiftly from the saddle and took cover as a slug ripped his sleeve. 'Stop right there!' he yelled. He fired again, aiming at the ground just in front of the horses. The animals shied. One of the men slipped sideways and fell. The other pulled hard on the reins, swerving into the trees.

Neither of the men was about to give

up, thinking perhaps that this new prey would be more fun than the last. But they were young and inexperienced and no match for someone who had cut his teeth in battle.

Buck had moved swiftly and silently as soon as he had fired, so the men converged on to an empty space.

'Throw your guns down!' Buck kept his voice calm, but its authority could not be mistaken.

A volley answered him, but he had moved again and had sight of his adversaries. He fired once again, this time aiming at the fleshy part of a leg. The yell of anguish that followed showed that he had hit his target.

Shifting his position once more, he repeated his order. 'Guns on the ground! You've had your last warning.'

There was silence.

'I've no quarrel with you,' Buck called. 'Couldn't stand aside an' let you harass a young lady. Go back where you came from an' that's the end of the matter.'

'Ya've no call to be interferin',' the

4

answer came back, aggressive and loud.

Buck had expected nothing less. By this time he had come up behind them and stepped out into the open. 'I told you to shuck your weapons,' he said quietly. 'Let's do this easy, then you can go on your way. We can end this here and now. Nobody else gets hurt.'

The men froze, dropped their guns on the ground and turned. 'Who in tarnation are you?' one of them snarled. 'We don't like strangers round these parts, 'specially when they interfere with our fun.'

'Don't matter none who I am,' Buck grated. 'I jus' don't cotton to scaring young ladies. So, if it's all the same to you, I suggest you go visit the doc, get that wound seen to. Leave your guns. I'll drop 'em at the sheriff's an' you can pick 'em up later.' He gestured towards their horses with his Colt. 'Get going afore I change my mind. An' next time pick on someone who can fight back.'

The young men, one of them holding a bandanna over his wound, remounted and rode quickly away with a final shouted, 'Ya've no idea who you're dealing with. We're gonna kill you!'

Buck watched them go, gathered up their hardware, and cursed himself for being a fool. This was not how he had wanted to start over in a new town.

He swung into the saddle and, remaining alert, headed for Rymansville.

He was weary, hot and more than ready for a cold beer and a hot bath. His clothes were dusty from the trail, his horse in need of a rest.

His eyes darted from left to right as he made his way along the rutted main drag, but it seemed that the worthy inhabitants had no more than a passing interest in the stranger who had entered their town, some acknowledging him with a brief nod of the head.

Halfway along the street he spied the buggy he had last seen hurtling along the trail. He hitched his horse next to it, slid from the saddle and waited. The young lady who emerged from the store carrying a heavy sack took his breath away. She was younger than he had imagined from the brief glimpse he'd had of her, no more than twenty-four he guessed, with an unspoiled beauty and a smile that could set men's pulses racing.

But she was directing her smile at the storekeeper, not at him, as he stepped forward to take the sack from her.

Recognition flared in her eyes. 'You!' she breathed.

'Me,' he agreed, touching his hat and swinging the sack on to the back of the buggy. 'Name's Buck, at your service. Just enquiring after your health after the run-in you had with those two wild young men.'

'My health's fine,' she said. 'I guess your intentions were to help back there, and I appreciate that, but you've only made matters worse by interfering. Those wild young men, as you call them, like to show off, but up till now that's as far as it's gone. What happened to them?'

Buck, taken aback by her attitude, said, 'I had to put a slug in one of them to slow 'em down, but just a flesh wound, no great harm done.'

'We'll have to wait and see what harm

you've done. If you take my advice, which I doubt you will, I suggest you watch your back while you're in town. Those boys think they're all-powerful, considering who their pa is.'

'My apologies, ma'am,' Buck said, 'if I've caused you any trouble. I wish you good day.'

She nodded. 'Thank you.'

'But first may I ask your name?'

'You may.'

He might have imagined the briefest smile of amusement touching the corner of the young lady's lips. He hoped so, although he doubted that he had made a good first impression.

'And your name, ma'am, if you please?'

'Sam Merryman. I own the homestead off the Ryman trail. You would have passed it as you came into town.'

This was more than he had asked for. 'Thank you, ma'am. It's been a pleasure talkin' to you.'

He touched the rim of his Stetson and turned to unhitch his horse.

He stepped into the saddle and made

his way slowly further down the street where a sign announced the presence of a saloon, the Winning Hand. Outside was a water trough where he allowed his mount to drink before he stepped inside to quench his own thirst.

'Be back afore you know it,' he said.

He mounted the three steps to the boardwalk and placed his hands on the batwings. He glanced round as he heard a loud and angry voice from the other side of the street. Outside one of the stores a woman was hoisting a crate on to the back of a wagon, while a heavyset man with a red face and a cruel twist to his mouth was angrily cursing her for being slow.

Buck shook his head. He had already interfered enough with matters that didn't concern him and received little thanks for it. Now was the time to ignore any other ladies in distress. He reluctantly withdrew his hands from the doors, stepped down into the street and walked slowly across to where the woman was struggling with another load.

He reckoned she was perhaps about thirty-five or so years old and could have been quite pretty, but her hair was untidy and her face a mite pinched. Her dress, too, had seen better days. The man, on the other hand, was clearly not underfed and, at that moment, was clasping a glass of beer in one hand.

Buck approached and touched his Stetson. Without a word he took hold of the wooden crate and placed it on the wagon. A second crate he handled in the same way. The woman treated him to a sweet smile.

'No trouble, ma'am,' he said.

A rough hand grasped him by the shoulder and swung him round to face the man who, Buck guessed, was the woman's husband.

'Best mind yer own business,' the man growled. 'This here's my wife, Sarah, an' she don't want help from no one.' He had retained his hold of the beer.

Buck shook himself free. 'Not how I saw it.'

'Ya saw it wrong.'

Buck figured the man was ready for a fight but he was unwilling to oblige. He backed away. 'Then accept my apologies.'

The man advanced towards him and it seemed that Buck's good intentions were going to end up with a brawl in the street.

'Baff,' Sarah pleaded with her husband. 'The man was only trying to help. Let's get back to the farm before it rains.'

Baff grunted and raised the glass to his lips, draining it of its contents.

Buck took the opportunity to step away. 'Happy to be of service, ma'am.' He touched his hat again and walked back to the saloon, half-expecting Baff's heavy hand to descend on him again. He was relieved when he reached the batwings unmolested.

2

Sam had watched Buck after he left her. She saw him turn and cross the road to where her friend, Sarah, was having difficulty loading up the wagon while her husband stood by.

You really are a knight in shining armour, Buck, she thought. *Seems to me you're going to find trouble sooner or later.*

She continued to look, drew in her breath as Baff grasped him. She made a step towards them. She knew what Baff was like and she thought it possible that she could prevent a fight. She didn't expect Buck to back away and she knew that Baff wouldn't.

But Buck did back off, and she kept her gaze on both men until Buck strode away. She wasn't sure what to make of it all. Baff was a large and intimidating man, but Buck seemed to be the sort of person who could look after himself. She chewed on her lip, wondering whether Buck's action in trying to help had made her life more difficult, and maybe Sarah's also.

She tried to shrug it off as she walked down to the hotel where Walt Grayson, the rancher, had a room he used as an office when in town. She nodded to Ma Finnigan and mounted the stairs.

A man with a deadpan expression stood silently outside a door marked 'Private'. She tried to avoid his lecherous gaze. 'The rancher's expecting me,' she said. She knocked.

Walt Grayson's authoritative voice reached her easily and, taking a deep breath, she walked into the room which was lit by two kerosene lamps hanging on ornate brackets. Here were all the signs of comfort and wealth. The room was furnished as both office and bedroom, though the bed was shielded from the rest of the room by a Chinese screen. All the furnishings and fittings looked very expensive, as might be expected of someone as self-important as this man. Pictures in gilt frames hung on the walls.

'Ah, Sam,' Walt said. 'I'm so glad you could come.' He was in his early forties, five feet ten inches, clean-shaven, with hair that showed no signs of grey. His eyes were a deep blue, set back below heavy brows. He took a long, fat cigar from a pouch, cut the end and lit it. 'West Indian,' he said. 'Specially imported.' He took several slow, satisfying pulls.

'I had a message you wanted to see me,' Sam said. 'Will this take long?'

'I hope not.' Walt rubbed his ear. 'Forgive me for speaking bluntly, but just lately I've felt a certain coldness in our relationship, Sam. I hope that isn't so.'

'We have no relationship, Walt,' Sam said quietly.

She took a seat, but chose an upright hardback rather than the soft leather-upholstered armchair. 'What is it that you wanted to see me about?'

'Straight to the point! That's what I like about you, Sam. You're very direct. I admire that. Very well, but at least allow me to offer you a glass of whiskey, the very best.'

'I've no doubt of that.'

'It's more civilized to discuss matters of importance over a good drink.' He poured the liquor from a cut-glass decanter into two matching glasses and held one out for her.

She accepted the glass and held it without putting it to her lips. 'Thanks,' she said, but did not intend to drink it. All the same she took a small sip. The liquor was smooth with a lingering aftertaste. 'I'd appreciate keeping this meeting as brief as possible, Walt. I have a homestead to look after and it won't run itself.'

'Of course. That's the point, isn't it? A homestead is so much of a responsibility for a young woman, if you don't mind me saying so.'

'I do mind,' Sam said. 'My husband ran it successfully when he was alive, and he taught me everything. He would want me to carry on the work he started.'

Walt blew smoke up to the ceiling and watched it hang in the still air. 'Sam, I don't want you to think I have any quarrel with you. We could so easily come to an understanding.'

'What sort of understanding?' Sam asked, although she thought she knew exactly what was in his mind.

He studied the glowing tip of his cigar. 'You're a beautiful woman, Sam. You must know that. And I'm a rich man. I have a large ranch and I intend to make it bigger. Size is everything out here.' He rose and moved closer. 'Together there's no limit to what we could achieve. I'm respected in this town.'

Sam had to smile at that. 'You own the town.'

Walt was not in the least put out. 'That, too. Folk make good money from me.'

Sam shifted in her seat. 'Walt, I understand that you would like to take over my land. It's good land, good pasture, plentiful supply of water. You've made an offer to buy it and I've said no. Please accept that answer.'

'A generous offer.'

'I won't deny that. Trouble is, I don't

16

want to sell.'

He appeared to be unaffected by her directness, dragged a chair close and sat down facing her. 'Then marry me. The best of both worlds.'

Sam had to admit to herself that Walt Grayson was a good-looking man, and a very wealthy one. He would certainly make a good catch for some woman.

'I've already given you my answer, Walt, and I haven't changed my mind. You're an attractive man. There's many a woman who would be pleased to be your wife. But I'm not ready to marry again.'

The rancher shrugged, as if being happy was not his measure of being a success. 'All I'm asking is for us to join forces. There's security in being big. You must see that. It's in both our interests for us to be man and wife. You've known for some time how I feel about you, and you've had plenty of time to think about it. It's not every day a woman gets an offer like this.' He laid his hand on her knee.

She flinched, but didn't much mind if

he noticed. 'I've thought about it, Walt, and the answer is the same as it's always been.'

'I'm a patient man, Sam,' Walt said. 'But I must extend my land soon.' He rose and refilled his glass. 'I need your access to water if I'm to build up my herd. I am also about to make a good offer for the plot occupied by Baff Finney. I'm certain he'll sell. When he does, your own land will be less valuable. I'm sure you will understand that.'

'I thought that farm belonged to his wife, Sarah,' Sam said.

Walt shrugged. Ash fell from his cigar on to the carpet. He flicked it with his toe. 'Technically, yes. But I've learned in life that you take what you want.'

If Sam had been hoping to see some good in him tonight she hadn't found it. 'Please don't try to scare me just because I'm a woman,' she said. 'I've given you my answer.'

'I like spirit in a woman, but too much can lead to serious consequences.'

That was the closest he had ever

come to an open warning, and Sam felt strongly that this was not going to be the end of the matter. She placed her glass on the marble-topped table and rose to her feet.

'I understand perfectly what you are telling me, Walt. I hope we can continue to be good neighbours. I am no danger to you. I really hope you are no threat to me.'

The rancher seemed genuinely surprised. 'None at all, Sam, I can assure you. I've laid my cards on the table. I've made a generous offer to you and I'll increase it in the expectation that you will change your mind before long.'

He took her arm, and guided her across the room as if she needed help. 'Think about it, Sam. That's all I ask. But don't delay too long.'

He held the door open for her and spoke to the man on duty. 'See her safely to her horse, Larry.'

As she left, Sam wondered if she had done the right thing. The homestead was hard work, but she was making a go of it. Her husband would have been proud of her.

But could she possibly survive in this man's world?

3

Buck pushed open the batwings of the Winning Hand saloon and strolled up to the bar where a dozen or so men, cow-punchers mainly, were filling their bellies at the end of a long day.

'Cold beer,' he said to the barkeep, a small jovial man, bald as a snake's head. 'I gotta throat like a hog's back.'

'All our beer's cold,' the barkeep told him and set the glass in front of him.

As Buck gratefully took a drink from the refreshing liquid he gazed around. There was the usual assortment of patrons, all with a glass in front of them, some at gambling tables, others with their arm round the waists of the doves.

As he looked he noticed with some concern that one of the men at a side table was giving him a hard look and was leaving the saloon with some haste. As he looked closer he saw that the other men at the table were glancing at him and whispering together.

'Travelled far?' the barkeep asked.

'Far enough.'

'Stayin' in town?'

'Where d'you recommend?' Buck asked.

The man smiled. 'No problem there. There's only one hotel. The Watering Hole, just a ways down. You'll be comfortable at Ma Finnigan's.'

Buck nodded his thanks, drained his glass and pushed it across for a refill. At that moment he felt a painful grip on his shoulder and he was swung violently round to face a large man with the appearance of a grizzly. Small, red-rimmed eyes glared out from a whiskered face, the mouth now set in a snarl.

'Ya ain't going nowhere 'cept on yer way,' the Bear growled.

Buck grabbed at the hand with a strength no less than that of the other man, twisted the fingers back until he felt a bone snap.

The Bear swore, released his grip and,

with his other hand, immediately took a swing.

Buck swayed back. 'Don't take kindly to bein' handled in that way,' he rasped and brought his fist up into his assailant's jaw. It had little effect, as his knuckles felt they had struck rock. A solid punch took him on the shoulder and for a moment, as he tried to ride the blow, he was caught off balance. Before he could recover another iron fist hit him on the side of his head, briefly blurring his vision and making his senses reel. As he staggered back he came up against the bar which saved him from ending up on the floor.

This wasn't going well. With an effort he pushed himself away and attacked with a whirlwind of punches, most of which landed somewhere and gave him some respite. The other men at the bar had stepped away, leaving space for the fight to continue.

Buck and the Bear circled one another, each respectful of his opponent and aware that one good strike could end the contest.

'Why're ya doing this?' Buck gasped.

'Ya shot Jas fer no reason an' yer gonna pay for that. Nobody hurts the boss's son an' gets away with it.'

Buck suddenly realized what this was all about. Out of the corner of his eye he saw one of the young men he had confronted earlier.

'You do their fighting for them, eh?' Buck said. 'Have you asked them why I had to loose off a shot? Have you asked them what they were doing?'

'Naw, an' I don't intend to,' Bear said. He rushed forward, arms swinging, but was met by a solid right to the nose. Blood spurted. 'I'll kill ya for that!' He bore in again, but Buck was light on his feet, intent on avoiding being crushed by those muscular arms.

'I've had a long day,' Buck grated. 'We can share a bottle. Whadya say?'

The Bear grinned wickedly. 'We've done talkin'. Yer gonna wish ya hadn't set foot in this town.'

He leaped forward with surprising speed, wrapped his arms around Buck's

24

body and squeezed. Buck was now facing away from his opponent and felt hot breath on his neck. He could hardly breathe as the air was squashed out of his chest.

'Goddamn it!' he gasped. 'You've picked on the wrong man.' He jerked his head back violently and heard the crack as the Bear's nose broke. The pressure eased slightly. Buck took hold of two of the Bear's fingers and bent them back until they too snapped.

The Bear certainly felt that, for he released his hold altogether, stepped back and put one hand up to his face where blood was pouring down into his mouth. He glared down at his broken fingers. Madness flared in his eyes. A noise like that of a wounded animal escaped his lips.

This time the Bear's attack, fuelled by anger, was more undisciplined and Buck found it easy to dodge and sway so that most punches went wide. When the chance came he swung hard and connected with the side of the Bear's head. The man staggered sideways, knocked into a chair and fell against a table. The table gave way and the Bear sat down heavily.

He was soon on his feet again and Buck retreated, seeing his opponent's hand drop down to his six-gun. The last thing Buck wanted was to be involved in a gun fight. He drew his own Colt with a blur of motion.

'Enough!' he said, keeping his voice even. 'Let's stop this right now. I've got an appointment for a meal and a bath and a good night's sleep. I'm not looking for trouble. Join me with that bottle. That must be better than fighting.'

For the space of several seconds time seemed to stand still. The Bear's gun was halfway out of its holster. If he had continued the draw Buck would have had no choice but to pull the trigger.

'There's no need for this,' Buck said. 'You've made your point. I'm gonna finish my drink, then I'll leave.'

A voice behind said, 'I've gotta better idea. Can't speak for the comfort the law kin offer, though. Bed's a mite hard and the food's not so good, but you won't be disturbed none. Now, both o' you varmints put the hardware away. I got business with this man here.'

Buck whirled. A tall, bearded man stood about three feet away. There was a weary smile on his face, a silver star on his shirt and a Colt in his hand.

'You're disturbing the peace,' the lawman said. 'And in this town that's agin the law. Till sundown anyways,' he added. 'Let's go find out what the jail can offer. Think it's time we got better acquainted.'

Buck had sense enough to holster his Colt as he lifted his glass and drained it. 'What in tarnation …?'

'Shuck yer gun. Careful. Lay it on the bar.'

Buck hesitated, but only briefly. Much better to stay alive and sort out this misunderstanding later than to upset the trigger finger of the lawman. He took out his gun with thumb and finger and laid it on the polished wood.

'Look after that for me,' he said as the barkeep scooped up the weapon. 'I'll be back.'

'Wouldn't count on it,' the marshal grated. 'Now, walk in front of me and we'll have a chat down at the office. My finger's a mite itchy, so don't try anything.'

Buck shrugged. 'Dunno what your problem is, but you're making a mistake.'

'The mistake was yours when you rode into my town. Now, git moving.' Without taking his eyes off Buck the lawman waved his gun at the Bear. 'Any more disturbance from you and there'll be two in the cells tonight.'

'I ain't done nothin', Marshal,' the Bear said.

Buck preceded the marshal out through the batwings and into the street. He was conscious of the gun at his back and of the curious stares from the good folk of the town as he strode purposefully to the law office.

The lawman didn't speak again until they were inside and he had taken up position behind his desk with his Colt resting within easy reach. Buck sat, relaxed, in an upright chair.

'Name's Casey Humble,' the lawman

said. 'I'm marshal in this town.' He took a swig from a glass of the whiskey he had clearly been enjoying when he had been interrupted. 'Mebbe you'd care to tell me what name you're going by today.'

Buck eyed the liquor, which apparently was not going to be offered to him. 'Can't say as I know what this is about,' he said. 'Don't know who you think I am, but I've had the same name for the past twenty-seven years an' I don't intend to change it.'

The marshal shrugged. 'P'raps you'd share that information with me, then we can get down to the reason for your visit.'

'Buck Norris.'

'Good as any other, I reckon. What's the reason for coming to Rymansville?'

'Lookin' for work. I can turn my hand to most things.'

'Yeah?'

'Tried to make a fortune. Ran wild for a bit. Had a spell as a lawman.'

'Were ya any good at it?'

'Had my moments. You lookin' for a deputy?'

'Got me a good one.'

Buck said, 'Dangerous job. Not paid enough in my book.'

This brought a loud guffaw from the marshal. 'That why you changed sides?'

Buck was losing the trend of the questions. 'Don't know what you mean, Marshal.'

'Bein' an outlaw is not a profession that's looked upon with any great tolerance, Buck, if that's what you like to call yourself. I s'pose you reckoned you wouldn't be recognized here? If so you would've been well advised to move on through. We may be a small place but we keep ourselves well informed.'

Buck levered himself from his chair. 'Right, Marshal, I'm obliged. I don't know what you're talking about, but now that's settled I need to see to my horse, fill my belly and get some shut-eye. You wouldn't expect me to leave before sunup?'

The marshal grabbed his gun. 'Siddown! You're not going anywhere, 'cept back there.' He jerked his thumb.

'There's a nice warm cell waitin' fer you.'

'What the hell for?' Buck sat again, reluctantly.

By way of an answer Casey Humble reached over to a shelf and took down a poster which he spread out on the desk. 'Good likeness, eh?'

'It's upside down, Marshal,' Buck said, but he had a good idea what the poster showed. It also offered $5,000 reward for the capture of the outlaw, Ray Norris.

'Don't play games,' Casey growled, but turned the poster round. 'Know who that is?'

Buck did, and his heart gave a leap. He recognized his brother immediately. Whoever had drawn the portrait had made a good job of it. 'Yeah. Sorta looks like me.'

'Not only looks like you. It is you.'

'There's many folk look like me,' Buck said. 'But that ain't me.'

The lawman raised his eyebrows. 'You might as well come clean. Mebbe the judge'll go easy on you.'

4

'OK, Marshal, I guess I gotta tell you the truth. That picture there is my brother, Ray. Or it certainly looks like him. I haven't seen him since we fought together in '63. He went chasin' after the killers of our ma and pa. I should've done the same. He was gonna follow me to Denver.'

As he spoke he felt the familiar pang of guilt as he recalled how he had parted from his brother after their farm had been razed to the ground.

'We were young then,' Buck continued. 'Sixteen and seventeen. We'd witnessed things nobody at that age should see.'

'Go on,' the marshal said. 'This gets interesting.'

'Yeah,' Buck growled. 'But interestin' ain't the word I'd use. If that's his picture, an' it sure looks like it, he must've turned outlaw. If so, I figure he must've been driven to it. I ain't heard nothin' of him for the past eleven years.'

Casey let out a roar of amusement. 'That's the best I've heard for a long time. Your brother, eh? So, I let you go and then the law goes chasing after him. Meantime you get on with yer robbin' an' killin'. If that's your idea I don't cotton to it.'

'We parted company like I told you. That's why I've been travellin' for all those years past, hoping to strike it rich.'

'An' did you make yer fortune?'

Buck slapped his pants. The dust of the trail filled the air. 'Don't appear so. Given up on that idea. I reckon I'll settle for a peaceful life from here on.'

'You ain't made much of a good start.' Casey had clearly had enough. 'Now, I'm a busy man. I've heard plenty, so if you don't mind I'll git you settled. On yer feet!'

With the marshal's Colt pointing steadily at him Buck had no choice. He walked ahead of the marshal and watched with a sinking heart as the lock clicked on his cell door.

He grasped the bars. 'You're making a big mistake, Marshal.'

'We'll see what the judge has to say when he gits here.'

'When'll that be?'

'Next week, but don't let that bother you.'

'It does bother me. What about my horse and belongings?'

The marshal showed some impatience. 'Your horse'll be put in the livery. Of course,' he smiled for the first time, 'all expenses for that and for board and lodging will be taken from any assets you may be carryin'. Can't expect the town to pay.' He turned and left.

He was soon back. 'Oh, and you'll have to pay for the damage you did in the saloon. Hope you got sufficient.' With that he slammed the door behind him, leaving Buck alone.

'Dammit!' Buck growled. He eyed the contents of his cell; a cot fixed to the floor, a dirty jug, a tin mug and a receptacle for his needs. This wasn't the welcome he had hoped for.

He climbed on to the cot and stretched up. From that position he allowed the coolness of the late breeze to brush his face as he listened to the clatter of horses' hoofs and the indistinct murmur of human voices out in the main street.

None of these sounds was reassuring.

'Marshal!' he yelled. 'I want outta here.' He didn't expect a response, and he didn't get one. 'Marshal, I'm hungry.' He rattled the tin mug along the metal bars.

This had the effect of bringing the lawman from his office, a scowl the size of a barn door on his face.

'Any more noise outta you and you'll go without food till morning. Anyway, not much point in feedin' you too well. Don't reckon a full belly will be much use in the here-after.'

Buck gripped the bars until his knuckles were white. 'Marshal, I've been trying to tell you. You've got the wrong man.'

The marshal sighed. 'Yeah, I've bin told that afore, more times than fleas on a hound. Now, shuddup an' let me get on with my work.'

'OK, Marshal,' Buck said, trying to inject a little humility into his voice. 'You've got your duties to attend to, but that surely doesn't include starving your prisoners to death. It's been a long day.'

The marshal's attitude seemed to soften. 'Yeah. I'll get something sent down from Maisie's Eating House in a while.'

'Thanks, Marshal.' He considered asking for a beer, but thought better of it.

Casey seemed inclined to linger, leaning against the wall and firing up a stogie. 'D'ya sleep well?' he asked.

Buck, surprised at the question, eyed the basic sleeping arrangements in the cell. 'Yeah,' he said, 'but if you're offering something a mite more comfortable I'll thank you.'

Casey found this amusing. 'Nope, no chance of that. You'll need to make do with what the town provides. You may hear some gunfire during the night. Don't let it worry you.'

'Expecting trouble?'

'Nothin' I cain't handle. Just thought I'd let you know in case you're the worryin' kind.'

'Thanks, Marshal. The thing I worry about is getting outta here and fillin' my belly.'

Buck wondered whether Casey Humble was a man of his word, but it turned out that he was. A hot meal of beef stew and crusty bread, washed down with water was very welcome and he finished the lot.

As he ate, Casey stayed, watching him closely. 'You don't act like an outlaw,' he said.

'How do outlaws act?'

'Dunno, but I've met a lotta wild men during my term in office an' they all had somethin' about them that showed them for what they were.'

Between mouthfuls Buck said, 'Met a couple of ladies earlier on.' He described them. 'Who were they?'

'Why d'ya wanna know?'

'Interested, Marshal. 'S all.'

'I heard about Sam an' the way you

stopped the two rancher's boys. One of 'em was sayin' how you nearly shot his leg off. Is that what the fight in the saloon was about?'

Buck nodded. 'Reckon so. Who is she?'

'Sam Merryman. Runs a homestead. Husband died not far back. Purty young woman. Catches the eyes of many of the young men.'

'And the other one?'

For a moment there was a wistful look in the marshal's eyes. 'That'd be Sarah. Married to Baff. He oughta be locked up, but I got nothing to lock him up for.'

Buck cleared his plate and handed it back through the bars. 'You've got nothing to lock me up for, but that didn't stop you.'

'I'm workin' on it.'

'I told you I'm no outlaw.'

'So you did,' the marshal said, and left.

After that Buck managed to sleep fitfully until he was awakened by an early breakfast, brought in by a deputy.

'Appreciate it,' he said and tucked in. After all, he might as well enjoy it since it was all going on his bill.

Sometime after that he heard a noise coming from the office. The light coming through the cell window told him the day was advancing. No doubt the splendid lawman had been busy and had made another arrest. Maybe it would be good to have a little company.

When the door opened he was surprised to see that his visitor was a small, rat-faced man dressed in black vest and jeans who was jangling a bunch of keys in one hand. An ivory-handled Colt was in the other.

'This is yer lucky day,' the man said, inserting the key in the lock and swinging the cell door open. 'Reckon the marshal was gonna see you hang.'

Buck stepped out of his cell. 'Who the hell are you?'

'Clint's the name. Come to git ya out.'

Buck didn't wait for explanations. They could wait until later. He followed his unexpected rescuer through into the outer office where he saw that the marshal had been bound and gagged and secured to his chair by rope. A cut across his forehead was oozing blood.

'D'ya want me to kill him?' Clint asked, pointing his gun at the marshal's head.

Buck made pretence of considering the question. 'Naw, he ain't worth the lead. Anyways, there's no call to draw attention to ourselves.'

Clint holstered his weapon. 'I could do it quiet.' From his boot he slid out a thin-bladed knife. 'Just say the word.'

Buck shook his head. 'He ain't gonna give us any trouble. Are you, Marshal?'

He grinned down at the unhappy lawman, reached over and drained the glass of whiskey the marshal had been about to enjoy. 'I reckon his standing's not gonna be too high when folk learn that he's lost a very dangerous prisoner.'

Clint laughed, a tinny, whistling sound through bad teeth. 'I git yer meaning. He'll allus be the marshal who let Ray Norris slip through his fingers. He'll never live it down. I gotta hand it to ya, Ray, ya sure are a mean *hombre*.'

'Yeah,' Buck muttered. 'I sure am, ain't I?'

'What I cain't reckon,' Clint said, 'is how come ya let him catch ya in the first place.'

'I was dreaming,' Buck said. 'Thinkin' I might be able to settle down here in Rymansville. Thought nobody'd cotton on to who I was. Mebbe make my fortune. Every man can dream, I reckon.'

'Yeah,' Clint said. 'Glad I happened along, though I reckon you'd've given 'em the slip soon enough.'

Buck nodded and grinned. 'I was workin' on it.'

He turned his gaze on the hapless marshal whose eyes were smouldering with anger. 'Got me a free meal and a bed for the night. Casey here ain't too smart, but he treated me well enough, so I wouldn't want to end his career just yet.'

'Whatever ya say.' Clint reluctantly sheathed his knife, running his hands through his hair. 'Cain't b'lieve I rescued Ray Norris.'

'The trouble with that is, I ain't...'

Buck began, then stopped in mid-sentence, as he visualized the effect that would have on his rescuer. 'I ain't sorry you did, either. Let's get outta here.'

'Where's yer gun?' Clint asked.

'Left it in the saloon.' Buck walked around the desk and opened one of the drawers. He reached in and withdrew a Colt .45 that looked as if it had seen better days. 'This'll do. Hope you don't mind,' he said to Casey. 'You kin have the one I left with the barkeep. Reckon you've got the best of the deal. OK?'

Taking a series of grunts as assent, he smiled broadly, gathered up some shells and slipped the gun into his holster.

With a last glance at the lawman he allowed Clint to lead the way out into the street. They proceeded cautiously, but nobody appeared to take much notice.

Two horses were hitched to the rail, one of them Buck's own chestnut. They climbed into the saddles and turned their mounts to head west, the fastest way out of town.

5

After Buck and Clint had left Casey struggled with his bonds. But Clint had done a good job and the knots would not yield. Neither could Casey slip the ropes from his limbs. The worst thing was that Clint had tied him to the chair.

He eyed the empty glass, the contents of which had found its way down Buck's throat. The anger he felt at that final insult gave him the determination for revenge.

'Damn you! Both of ya! I'll get you an' I'll lock you up till you're old.'

A few further curses escaped his lips while he considered what options he had. At least his feet were on the floor. Although the chair was heavy he managed with a series of jerky movements to move it from behind the desk and make some progress towards the door. The fact that it was closed made him pause while he worked out how he was going to open it.

But what would happen if he succeeded? He, the marshal of Rymansville, would be sitting in the open doorway, still bound and helpless, the butt of jokes at best. At worst, some varmint might take a shot at him.

It was at that moment of indecision that he heard the gunfire from further up the street. The firing seemed to have some purpose, to be less random than when the cowboys in the saloon had gone wild. There was also the fact that this was happening during the day, when the town should have been quiet.

He knew with certainty that something was wrong and that he was needed. He redoubled his efforts to free himself. As he struggled the door burst open with such force that it knocked him over backwards. For a moment the chair teetered, but then he fell and the back of his head hit the floor hard. He let out a howl of anger.

The young man who now stood in the

doorway, and who had been the cause of his pain, pushed his way into the room and stared.

'What ...'

'Don't just stand there,' Casey grated. 'Git me up an' untie me.'

Jesse France, the deputy marshal, a young fresh-faced man with a shock of unruly hair, gathered himself together swiftly. He hoisted the chair upright and went to work on the bonds.

'What the hell happened to you?' he asked.

'What's goin' on out in the street?' Casey growled as the ropes fell away.

'That's what I came to tell you,' Jesse said. 'The bank's bein' robbed.'

'Then whadya doing here? Git back down there.'

Jesse hurried away while Casey grabbed the shotgun from the cabinet, loaded it, checked his Colt, and ran after his deputy. When he reached the bank he saw with some satisfaction that the robbers were holed up inside.

In the dust of the main drag lay a body,

unmoving.

'Who's the lucky man?' Casey asked.

Jesse chuckled. 'Dunno. We can't get close enough to find out who he is.'

Casey peered and noticed that the robber was wearing a bandanna over his face. 'Guess they're all feelin' the need not to be recognized, eh?'

'Looks that way,' Jesse agreed.

'How many inside?'

'Three of 'em,' Jesse told him. 'Their horses were out back, but we managed to lead them away. These *hombres* don't seem ready to give up.'

Casey nodded as a fusillade of shots came from the smashed window in the bank. 'Then why don't we go in after them? We have the fire power.' He had confidence in his deputy and realized there must be a reason why he was not returning fire.

'There's two hostages inside,' Jesse said. 'The robbers've threatened to kill them if we don't let them ride.'

'Who've they got?' Casey asked.

'Oswald, the manager, and one of his

clerks, young Landon.'

'They both got families, ain't they?' Casey said.

'Yeah. Billy Landon's just got wed.'

'Whadya reckon?'

'We gotta let 'em go,' Jesse said. 'That's why I came to get ya. Your decision.'

'You've done well, Jesse. Not got many options, have we?' He cupped his hands around his mouth and raised his voice. 'Come on out with yer hands up.'

An answering shout left him in no doubt of the robbers' intentions.

'I tried offering 'em a fair trial,' Jesse said. 'I got the same curses.'

'Then we gotta do something else.' Casey didn't have to ponder for long. 'Gimme something white,' he said. 'I'm gonna talk to 'em.'

Someone produced a pair of long johns and he held them aloft. 'Can't say they're very white,' he muttered, but he waved them above his head. 'I'm comin' over!' he shouted and strode forward. The firing stopped and an outlaw appeared on the steps of the bank. His face, too, was concealed behind his bandanna. Casey went forward until he was within six feet of the man.

'Looks like we've got us a stand-off,' he said, conversationally.

This brought a guffaw from the outlaw. 'It sure do, don't it?'

'Glad you agree. What're we gonna do about it?'

'Ya let us go. Simple.'

'Sounds good to me. OK. Tell your friends to show themselves. If the hostages haven't been harmed you can mount up an' go.'

'Easy as that?'

'Yep, easy as that. Less you wanna be like him.' Casey pointed to the body still lying in the dirt.

'We could kill you right now.'

'You ain't killed nobody so far.'

The outlaw laughed again. 'Nope.'

'Well, what're we waitin' fer?'

'We're takin' the hostages with us.'

'That's not part of the deal.'

The outlaw looked over Casey's head to where a small and angry crowd of men had gathered, most with guns. 'They'd shoot us down before we'd taken two steps.'

'Not if I tell 'em not to.'

'I gotta better idea. We take the hostages with us — an' the money.'

'That's not part of the deal, either.'

'Then we're back where we started. Ya'd best go before we start shootin'.'

'Give yerselves up,' Casey said. 'Save us all a loada trouble.'

'We ain't gonna do that, Marshal.'

'Then you'll die.'

'We won't be the only ones.'

Casey thought hard, trying to avoid the appearance of indecision. 'Right, this is my final offer. We bring your horses round, ready but without the saddle-bags. The bank's money stays in the bank, otherwise I might not be able to control the townsfolk. It's their money. They worked hard for it. Some of 'em might get ornery if they see you riding off with it. You release the hostages and shuck yer weapons. You stay an' you die.'

He held up his hand to forestall the

angry response from the outlaw. 'Instead of the two hostages you take me along with you.'

He paused. 'I'll give you a few minutes to talk to your friends.' He turned and walked steadily towards his deputy, expecting at any moment to hear the bark of a Colt or to feel hot lead in his back.

He gave instructions to Jesse, handed him his gunbelt and waited. Within minutes the same man appeared on the steps. Behind him the two hostages were pushed out and stood there silently while the other two robbers remained concealed.

'We agree.'

Casey smiled grimly. He looked hard at Jesse. 'You know what you have to do.' Then he walked to the centre of the road and stopped. The hostages were shoved roughly forward.

Oswald Breck, the manager, a short, amiable man with a round face, spoke quietly.

'You don't have to do this, Casey. They're not the nicest bunch of men I've ever met.'

'I know what I'm doing,' Casey said, knowing at the same time that it wasn't true.

Billy Landon still had fear in his eyes. He said, simply, 'Thanks, Marshal.'

'We ain't got all day!' the outlaw shouted. Casey walked on until he stood in front of the outlaw. He held out his hand.

'Is it a deal?' He gazed into the man's eyes.

After a brief hesitation the outlaw put out his own hand and they shook. Then Casey was grabbed and pulled inside the bank, where his hands were tied behind his back.

'Where's the horses?'

He needn't have asked as the sound of hoofs on the hard ground reached their ears. Four mounts came up, one of them the marshal's own.

'Walk ahead of us, Marshal,' one of the men said. 'If there's any shootin' the second shot will be the one that kills you.'

Casey nodded and, with a gun in his back, mounted up and rode out with the outlaws around him.

Nobody spoke to him until they were well clear of the town. Although he heard mutterings among the outlaws themselves, he was unable to make out what they were saying. He could, however, hazard a guess about their plans for his future from the way in which they looked at him. He tried not to dwell on the possibility of a rope round his neck.

'Where're we going?' he asked.

'You ain't goin' nowhere.' This from one of the men who hadn't yet spoken.

'What the hell's that s'posed to mean?'

The man chuckled but made no reply, so Casey concentrated on remembering the trail they were taking. After riding for half an hour, during which time the outlaws had constantly been searching their back trail for signs of being followed, they halted under the shelter of a stand of willow.

'Far enough,' one of the men growled. 'I say we shoot him here and now.'

'Waste of lead,' another said. 'I say we hang him.' He pointed to a sturdy branch.

For a moment Casey considered

making a run for it, but at the same time he knew he would be brought down before his horse was up to full speed, and without the use of his hands he would be at a great disadvantage.

He waited for the inevitable. At the very least he would try to put up a good fight.

But that was unnecessary. The outlaw who had shaken his hand said, 'I've shook on it. No hanging.' He turned his gaze on Casey. 'You can go.'

'How about untying me first?'

'Yer lucky to keep yer life. If we meet agin ya may not be so lucky.'

'I'll look forward to that. I figure it's you who'll be needin' the luck.' Casey turned his horse and dug his heels in.

He rode hard for half a mile, looking out for signs of his deputy. He was confident Jesse would not have let him down.

6

Buck and Clint rode slowly until they had reached the outskirts of the town so as not to arouse any unwanted attention. As gunfire sounded behind them Clint whipped his horse into a fast gallop. Buck kept up but glanced round several times to find out who was chasing them. To his surprise there was no sign of pursuit.

As they slowed again he rode abreast of Clint. 'What the hell was that all about? Reckoned we'd bin discovered.'

Clint's face broke into a grin. 'It's OK. All bin taken care of.'

'You know what the shootin' was?'

Clint's grin grew even broader. 'Good planning,' he said. 'Bank's just bein' robbed, that's all.'

'You mean my rescue and the robbery were arranged so they took place at the same time?'

Clint looked pleased with himself. 'Yep.

My idea. Didn't want a posse on our trail.'

'You seem to have thought of everything,' Buck said. He leaned over and held out his hand to his rescuer. 'I owe you. Hope our paths cross again sometime so I can pay you back.'

The look of pleasure on Clint's face quickly changed to one of suspicion. He didn't take the offered hand.

'What're you gonna to do? Thought we were pards now.'

Buck didn't take to that idea. 'Best if we go our own separate ways. They're sure to send a posse after me an' you'll be caught up in that. You've done me a great favour an' I won't forget.'

Clint shook his head hard. 'It don't work like that. Yeah, ya owe me an' you kin pay me back right now by joining our gang. We got skills but we're sorta short of men. You won't never regret it.'

Buck was regretting it already as he urged his horse into a trot. 'Truth is, Clint, I ain't ever had a gang. Not what you'd call a proper gang, anyway. Sure, I rode with some outlaws for a while but I left 'em behind when I set out for Colorado. Things were getting too hot. And I was planning to start a new career some place.'

Clint laughed. 'Men like you and me never change sides.' He slapped his thigh as an idea occurred to him. 'Naw, if you wanna start again I'm the man you want to help ya. Our leader got hisself shot a little while back. You're just the man to take his place.'

Buck was beginning to wonder if he would have been better off in jail. 'Nope. Reckon I'd be better on my own. Seems you'll need to look elsewhere for a leader.'

This time Clint's eyes narrowed and his face creased into a scowl. 'Ya don't git it, do ya? I saved yer life back there. They'd've hung ya fer sure. Yeah, ya owe me an' I'm callin' in that debt right now.'

Buck shrugged. Maybe Clint had a point. It wouldn't do any harm, he supposed, to go along with his rescuer for a while, see how things turned out.

'OK, Clint. I'll meet the boys, but I ain't committing myself to anything else.'

Clint appeared to accept this, but Buck sensed that the atmosphere between them had changed. They rode on in silence for the next forty minutes, aiming for what looked to Buck like a series of canyons set in the sides of a rocky fortress.

'Where're we going?' he asked.

'You'll see.' Clint smirked. 'Where they ain't gonna find us.'

They traversed hard, rocky ground, swinging left and right into the many canyons. Buck concentrated on keeping track. Then, without warning the sides opened out and Buck could see a few cabins and a small stream meandering through lush green grass.

'Told ya,' Clint said. 'There's nobody knows about this place. Come an' meet the boys. Some are away jus' now, but there's one or two still here.'

The first man they saw stepped out of one of the huts and planted himself in front of their mounts, causing them to haul on the reins.

'That there's Growler,' Clint told Buck, gesturing with his head. 'So called cos of the happy way he looks at things. Don't let that worry you none, though. He's a good man to have around.'

The man was large, barrel-chested with huge muscles showing through his shirt.

'Who's this?' he growled, pointing at Buck.

Clint grinned. 'This here's Ray Norris. Led a gang of his own. Got hisself tied up by the law in Rymansville. Reckoned he'd be an asset to us after Homer got shot.'

'Reckon I'd made my opinion clear,' Growler said. 'We don't want nobody else here. No sense in bringin' in a stranger.'

Buck said nothing, thinking it best to stay silent until he'd met the others, after which he could assess how he would handle the situation. He had to take control soon. It occurred to him that he had been a little unwise to allow himself to be brought here. If the men didn't believe he was who he was supposed to be they could very easily kill him and dispose of his body. It would never be found. And there was nobody to care.

As Growler stepped back into the hut

they continued on their way, a matter of about fifty yards, where Clint hitched his horse outside a larger building from which came the smell of cooking. Buck followed suit, suddenly realizing how hungry he was.

'We got us a good cook,' Clint explained. 'Ain't good fer much else, though.'

It was a while before they were getting ready to tackle the hot meal when three more riders came into the camp. Their horses had been ridden hard and were sweat-slicked. As the men dismounted outside Buck could hear them grumbling among themselves. Growler and Clint ran outside.

'Where's Frank?' Clint demanded when he noticed that only three men had returned.

'He won't be coming,' one man said. 'Fact is he ain't ever gonna come. We were out-gunned. Frank got hit afore we even knew we were being ambushed. Didn't have a chance.'

'An' the money?'

'Ain't got it. Had to leave in a hurry.

We were lucky to get away with our lives.'

'How in tarnation could this've happened? We ain't made a good haul fer long enough.' Clint seemed to be more upset over the loss of the loot than the death of one of the gang.

'Dunno,' another man said. 'But I darn well intend to find out.'

'Ya can tell us about it while we eat. Grub's ready.'

Around the table the tale was told. When it got to the point of their escape one of the men, with matted hair down past his shoulders, gazed hard at Clint.

'Thought you were s'posed to deal with the marshal.'

'Yeah, he was tied up good. My side of the plan went OK,' Clint said.

'How was it he was the one we hadda take as hostage?'

'Don't know nothin' about that, Yol. Me an' Ray here reckoned it was best not to kill him. Fact is we got us a new recruit, like I said I would.' He nodded in the direction of Buck. 'Ray Norris.'

There was silence while the men

assessed the new-comer with hostile gazes.

'Don't look so glum, boys. Frank would've got hisself killed sooner or later.'

Buck thought it was time he spoke up. 'Bank jobs need luck as well as good planning,' he said. 'They're tricky. The law'll always be expectin' a raid an' there'll be plenty of folk prepared to defend their cash with guns.'

'Nobody asked your opinion,' Yol said. He looked at Clint. 'This was your idea. Mebbe it's a good one, mebbe not. Ray Norris, you say?'

'Ran an outlaw gang till it got too hot for him,' Clint exaggerated. 'We lost Homer. Now you lost Frank. We need good men an' Ray wants to join.'

Buck felt five pairs of eyes inspecting him. 'I'm givin' it some thought,' he said.

Yol seemed to be the spokesman. 'Ya say you ran an outlaw gang? I guess you weren't all that successful.'

'Profitable enough,' Buck said. 'Made a good living from it, an' we didn't lose men like you seem to do.'

'We've had some bad luck jus' lately,' Yol said.

'So I believe.' Buck deliberately put a sneer into his voice.

'An' you didn't?'

'Like I said, the bigger the prize the greater the risk. But you can cut the risks by good planning an' pickin' your target.' He wondered whether he had overdone the criticism.

Yol levelled his gaze at the men, then switched it to stare at Buck. 'Care to share with us jus' how ya did that?'

Buck thought hard, drawing on his brief experience, mostly unsuccessful, as an outlaw. 'OK, I reckon you'd've robbed a stage at some time. Anyone got himself killed?'

Yol nodded. 'That's how we lost Billy.'

'Yeah. Figures. Time was when we walked away with ten thousand dollars without a shot bein' fired.' He paused to assess their interest.

'Yeah?'

'I got me a job as shotgun. Another of the gang, a woman of some years an' even more experience, rode as a passenger. She got herself ill during the journey an' the coach had to stop. While the driver gave her some help I helped myself to the contents of the strongbox. Easy. Nobody got hurt.'

'A woman!' Yol found that difficult to accept. 'We ain't never had a woman.'

'Wouldn't mind one, though,' someone said.

'More trouble than help,' Yol said.

The conversation continued until the sun had set, giving Buck no opportunity to escape. He yawned.

'I'm ready for bed,' he said. 'It's been a long day.'

'We'll talk agin in the morning,' Growler said, staring at Buck. 'I ain't made up my mind about you yet.'

'Suits me,' Buck said. 'I ain't made my mind up about you, either.'

As Clint walked with Buck to the sleeping quarters Buck said, 'Not too friendly, are they?'

'Give 'em time,' Clint told him. 'I was gonna fix you up with a bed, but ya might as well take Frank's now he won't be needing it no more.'

Buck was doubtful. 'The men mightn't be too keen on that,' he said. 'Seeing as how Frank's still warm in his grave.'

Clint shrugged. 'I reckon you kin handle yerself. Reckon there's time for a smoke before you settle yerself in?'

Buck made up his bunk and stowed his gear. Then he removed his saddle and bridle from his horse and led it to some rich pasture on the banks of the stream where it could crop to his heart's content. The night was warm with only a slight evening breeze. It was all quiet and deceptively peaceful as Buck and Clint sat on a rock, rolled the makings and struck a light to the ends.

Clint said suddenly. 'Fergot to tell ya, Ray. Sometime after sunup you'll be meetin' the last member of our gang. Name's Grant. Says he knew you over Kansas way some while back. Says he's lookin' forward to seein' you agin.'

'Can't wait,' Buck said. He didn't intend to.

They continued talking until they both decided to turn in for the night. Buck did not intend to sleep. If he could slip out of the camp quietly he would be well away before he was missed.

Clint's next words caused him to abandon his plans.

'You're safe here, Ray. We always post a sentry at night. Nobody can get in or out without bein' seen.'

'A comforting thought,' Buck said. Perhaps he could leave before Grant arrived in the morning. Perhaps Grant wouldn't remember Ray well. Perhaps Grant had got himself killed.

He slept well in spite of the uncertain answers to those questions.

7

Five minutes after leaving the outlaws Casey Humble was relieved to see his deputy emerge from behind an outcrop.

'Jesse! Am I pleased to see you! You did a great job. They never knew you were there.'

Jesse rode up to him, cut his bonds and handed him a gun and belt. They set off back towards town. 'I had you in my sights all the time, Casey,' he said. 'Reckoned they were gonna string you up. I'd've got two of 'em before they knew what was happening.'

'By which time I'd probably be dead,' Casey opined. 'Naw, you did the right thing, Jesse. Come sunup we'll get a posse together, see if we can't track 'em down. I reckon they're holed up somewhere. Not around here, though.' He gazed about him. 'They took me here on purpose.'

Jesse nodded in agreement. 'What're

you gonna do now?'

'Looking forward to a few cold beers. I'm gettin' too old for this.'

Jesse gave him a sideways glance. 'Sorry, Casey. There's something else you have to do before that.'

Casey sighed. 'Whatever it is you can deal with it.'

'Town council want to see you right away.'

'What in tarnation for?'

'Didn't say. Sounded urgent. The chairman in particular was in a bad mood. Caught me just as I was setting off. When I left he was in an even worse one.'

Casey sucked in his breath. 'OK, but set those beers up, Jesse. I'll deal with those chair-bound, self-opinionated varmints in no time at all.'

'What're you going to do about it, marshal?'

Samuel Sniper, chairman of the town council, stood solidly with feet planted well apart, hands resting on his big belly and with his thumbs hooked into his vest.

It was a stance he had taken pains to develop in an attempt to impress the good folk of Rymansville, although at five feet six inches and 155 pounds it could hardly be said that he was an imposing figure.

The marshal was not intimidated but, nevertheless, he thought it prudent to show some respect.

'I'm doing what I can, Chairman, but the situation's becoming harder to control.'

'We, that is to say, the townsfolk, pay you to protect our interests!' Milo Miles, owner of the bank, was tall, thin and gave the appearance of a hound on the scent. 'Our bank, robbed in broad daylight! What's going on?'

'I have to point out,' Casey said reasonably, 'that no robbery actually took place. The gang was stopped an' one of them was killed by my deputy at the time. Moreover, Oswald Breck an' young Billy Landon were unhurt.'

'While you, I understand, were tied up in your own office, I believe.' Ben Purdy, the gunsmith was almost enjoying Casey's discomfiture.

'Yeah,' Casey said. 'Things like that happen from time to time.'

'That may be so,' the chairman butted in. 'To come back to the point I was trying to make earlier, it seems to us that you are no longer in control an' we want to know whether you are still up to the job.'

'I reckon you've had no complaints so far,' Casey said, feeling that he was being unfairly criticized for something that was not his fault. 'What you're askin' me to do depends on a lotta things, 'specially how much liquor you serve up an' how much you're prepared to allow the shootings to go on in Rymansville.'

'What's changed, Casey?' James Marley, the saloon owner and the fourth member of the council, spoke for the first time. 'Been fine an' dandy so far. It's not just the attack on the bank, though that's bad enough, it's the fact that you seem to be losing your touch. You haven't got control of things.'

Casey, his anger rising, said, 'I ain't

lost my touch! What's happened is the boys from Walt Grayson's ranch have got to know that, even if I lock 'em up they'll be out afore I've even made out the paperwork.'

'Those boys can sure raise a thirst,' James agreed. He let out a roar of satisfaction. 'They can also keep the doves busy an' that's good for business.'

'Fact is,' Ben Purdy said, 'business is good for everyone. Of course the boys go wild from time to time. That's only natural with men like that. They spend what they get paid, an' if they didn't do it here in Rymansville they'd get rid of it some place else.'

'And we wouldn't like that,' Samuel Sniper said. 'None of us would.'

Milo Miles grunted approval. 'Makes sense,' he said. 'The store owners do well outta Walt Grayson an' his crew. I can vouch for that. The finances of many folk in this town are in a very satisfactory position.' He looked pointedly at Casey. 'You ain't done so bad yourself. You're paid above your station to keep things going smoothly. If you're getting too old for the job all you've gotta do is say so an' we'll find a younger man.'

Casey knew they could do just that, but he had plans to complete before he retired.

'I ain't ready to hang up my gun yet. Yeah, I've taken your money an' I've done what you asked. All I'm sayin' is that maybe a word with Walt Grayson may be a good idea.'

Samuel Sniper cleared his throat. 'I reckon you can leave the matter of the rancher to us. Your job is to keep the peace during the day and to allow the boys to let off steam a little at night, especially on pay day.' He smiled conspiratorially.

'Yeah,' Casey said. 'You make money while I'm the one who's likely to be shot at nigh on every day.'

'What're you complaining about, Casey?' The chairman brought an edge to his voice. 'Have you ever figured out why, with all the shootin' that goes on, the nearest you've come to being killed is when you got that slug in your leg?'

Casey had a good idea why, but he said, 'Been lucky, I guess.'

'No luck in it, Casey,' Samuel said. 'Walt Grayson is a generous man, but also a ruthless one. He pays his men well, but only if they keep in line. If they go beyond what he expects of them they pay a heavy price. Many of them would be made very welcome by the federal marshal. The boys let off steam, but when they point their pistols at you they shoot to miss.'

'Yup,' Ben Purdy butted in. 'We keep you alive an' we all make money.'

As they talked and consumed their liquor the sound of gunfire reached them.

'I kin hear the money jingling from here,' Casey said.

The chairman chortled, as if he felt better having let off a bit of steam.

'I reckon this calls for another drink.' He poured a good measure of Scotch whisky, a particularly pale blend, into five glasses. 'To the continuation of a happy state of affairs,' he said and raised his glass to his lips.

Casey accepted his glass, looked at it

and placed it on the table. 'If you don't mind, gentlemen,' he said, 'I'll just go and check on things.' He didn't wait for their reply as he strode to the door.

'Mind what we've been discussing,' Ben Purdy called after him, but Casey was already out of earshot.

He'd had enough. Things were going to change. He made his way to the law office, deep in thought. There he checked his Colt, unhooked the shotgun from the cabinet, took a mouthful of whiskey from his own bottle and walked purposefully towards the saloon, where the sound of gunfire was increasing. Time to put his authority to the test.

He took a deep breath and pushed his way through the batwings.

Inside, a small group of men, fired up by liquor, were pumping lead into the floor, the furniture and the ceiling. A man lay dead on the saloon floor. The ruckus was also spilling out on to the boardwalk and into the street.

He took in the scene at a glance, walked over to the dead man and turned him over with his foot. He recognized him at once as a married man who worked in the livery. The man had clearly not been carrying a gun.

Casey fired his shotgun into the air. Pieces of the roof floated down in the ensuing silence. He glared round at the angry faces.

'How did this man die?' he demanded, his voice holding all the pent-up frustration and anger that had been building up all day. This was going to be a severe test of how the gunmen would react to a newly strict hand of the law.

One of the men, a bully by the name of Tirrell, who was well known to Casey, stepped forward. 'Who wants to know?'

'The law wants to know. This man was unarmed. That's murder. How did it happen?'

'He must've stepped in the way of some lead.'

'From your gun?'

'Mebbe. Yeah. So what?'

'Then you're under arrest.' Casey gestured towards the door with the barrel of the shotgun. 'Jail for you.' He glared at the other gunmen, some of whom held their gun in one hand and a glass in the other. 'I'll want witnesses when I return. All of you can put your guns away now.'

None of them did.

'An' one of you go fetch the undertaker.' Casey couldn't tell whether anyone took on that duty. His eyes were fixed on Tirrell, who hadn't moved.

A grin stretched the man's mouth, showing uneven teeth.

'Best if ya leave while ya can still walk.' The large man glanced about him, seeking support. At a table four of his pards had been playing blackjack. They rose to their feet. Three others eased nearer, crowding the marshal. Casey held his ground.

'Ya gonna take us all on?' Tirrell sneered.

Casey settled his gaze on the man unflinchingly. 'Nope, reckon I couldn't do that. But if they make a false move you an' me, an' mebbe two of them, won't see the sun come up tomorrow. What's it to be?'

Tirrell took a moment to size up the situation, then sniggered.

'It's OK fellers. Go back to yer game. I kin handle this varmint.' He gave the marshal a venomous glare. 'Ya sorta have a death wish?'

Casey figured that perhaps he had, but nothing on his face showed what he was thinking. He firmed his jaw.

'Nope. Doin' my duty, 's all. I believe you killed this man an' you're gonna be judged for it. So, either you come with me now or go to meet your maker. I don't mind. Your call.'

Tirrell shrugged. 'Hard choice!'

'You sure you wanna stand up against me?'

For a brief moment doubt showed on Tirrell's face, then his grin returned.

'Sure do,' he said with an edge of triumph in his voice. ''Less ya wanna run with yer tail between yer legs like a cowardly cur.'

Casey wondered, not for the first time, why he was doing this. Tirrell, big and powerful, was also known to be fast on the draw.

'Outside, then. Rest of you stay where you are.' He angled so that he could keep the other men in his line of sight, then cautiously lowered his shotgun.

'What now?' Tirrell asked.

'We step outside. But first we shuck our pistols.' To the surprise of everyone, he withdrew his Colt with thumb and forefinger and laid it and the shotgun on the bar.

There was a gasp from the men. Tirrell stood undecided. 'What ya doing that fer?' he demanded.

Casey smiled as if at a child. 'If you're set on a fight I wanna give you a chance.' He indicated Tirrell's gun. 'Leave that next to mine an' join me outside.'

Before Tirrell could frame a reply Casey turned and walked out through the batwings into the dusk. He let his eyes become accustomed to the dim light.

When Tirrell emerged Casey saw that his gun still rested in its holster. He had taken a risk and it seemed he had failed.

But it wasn't over yet.

'Ya wanna fight me?' Tirrell asked as he stepped off the boardwalk to face the marshal. 'However ya wanna do it ya've made the wrong decision. I'm gonna kill ya.'

Casey was sure Tirrel meant what he said, but he didn't want to die just yet. He glanced back at the batwings where men were standing, anticipating the death of the town's marshal.

From the point of view of the onlookers there was to be only one outcome. Tirrell was well over six feet with muscles honed by hard work. In spite of his size he could move quickly.

Casey, on the other hand, was three inches shorter and was lighter by about fourteen pounds. The contest promised to be one-sided, and money quickly changed hands.

The two men stood ten paces apart, glaring at each other like gladiators.

'Got your blade on you?' Casey asked.

Tirrell nodded, suddenly understanding what Casey had in mind. His hand flipped aside his waistcoat to reveal the

Bowie knife at his left hip. It was a formidable weapon. He withdrew it and made several quick passes through the air. He advanced on the balls of his feet.

'I'm gonna slice you into little pieces,' he snarled. 'Where's yer own knife?'

'Here,' Casey said. He reached behind his head. The light from the saloon glinted on the slender blade of the throwing knife as it arced through the air. Tirrell saw it coming, but too late. The steel entered his chest and pierced his heart. He tried to speak as his hand instinctively flew down to his hip in an attempt to draw.

The Colt cleared leather but that was as far as it got before Tirrell's life was extinguished.

'That's the last draw you'll ever make,' Casey said with satisfaction.

But he wasn't out of danger.

He withdrew his second gun, which he had stuffed inside his shirt, but it wasn't necessary. From across the street a man holding a rifle emerged from a doorway. Casey recognized Jesse at once.

'Keep your hands away from your

belts,' Jesse shouted. 'First one to try anything smart gets the first slug. An' there'll be more where that came from.'

The men, hardcases maybe but also cowhands who valued their own lives, melted away. Jesse walked across the street.

'Sorta glad to see you,' Casey said.

Jesse grimaced. 'What the hell did you reckon you were doing, tangling with that lot?'

'Figured I had to prove a point,' Casey admitted.

'Wanna tell me all about it?'

'I need somethin' stronger than beer. I gotta bottle in my office. Needs opening.'

'Then let's git to it,' Jesse agreed as they watched the approach of the undertaker.

'Two bodies,' Casey told him. 'Mebbe more afore the night's through.'

When Jesse and the marshal were settled comfortably in the law office, each nursing a glass of liquor, Casey said, 'Town council reckon I'm fallin' down on my job.' He set about cleaning his guns.

'Are you?'

'Nope.'

'You've done everything they wanted, haven't you?'

'Yep, though it pains me to admit it. But that's about to change.'

Jesse raised his eyebrows, waiting for Casey to explain.

'Before I retire,' the marshal began, 'I wanna make this town safe for ordinary folk to go out at night. Walt Grayson an' his crowd have had the run of the place for too long. I aim to stir things up a bit, then I'll go an' get me a nice little house and grow flowers.'

Jesse's eyes glinted. 'Ya gotta nice little woman in mind to share it with?'

'None o' your concern.' Casey laughed, as the image of Sarah entered his mind. He stubbed out his cigar. 'Our glasses are empty. How did we let that happen?'

8

Buck was up early, hoping to ride out of the outlaws' camp without being challenged. He was disappointed to find that Clint was up before him. He lit up a stogie and drew smoke in deeply as he analysed his position. He had no intention of remaining with the outlaw gang, and every intention of staying alive.

Clint said, 'Grant should be here by now. He'll be mighty pleased to see a friendly face. Where did ya meet?'

Buck rubbed his chin. 'Can't rightly recall. Is he new to the gang?'

'Nope. Grant's been with us fer long enough. He works regular on the Grayson ranch. Good cover an' he gets to hear things.'

'Great,' Buck enthused, and hoped he sounded genuine.

Clint screwed his eyes against the glare of the early sun. 'This is him now.

Ya won't need no introduction I reckon. Let's go meet him.'

Buck walked with Clint towards the incoming rider. Buck had never seen him before, but put on a friendly smile as Grant drew near and dismounted.

'Ray wants to meet ya,' Clint called, then spoke to Grant in low tones that Buck could not hear. Eventually he said, 'I've told him what happened. Now I'll leave you two to talk old times.' He wandered off towards the hut from where the smell of bacon was filling the air.

Grant approached Buck and studied him carefully with a quizzical look. His eyes were small and mean. He had the appearance of a fit man of about thirty, with dark hair that he had allowed to grow long. His face was clean-shaven except for sideburns that nearly met under his chin.

'Surprised to see ya agin, Ray,' Grant said. 'You've changed a little since we last met.' He held out his hand.

'The years've done that,' Buck said, non-committally, accepting the handshake.

'But ya seemed to've taken care of yerself.'

'Don't live long in this business if you don't,' Buck said, relaxing slightly.

There was silence as each man sized the other up.

'Guess that's so,' Grant agreed. 'Recall last time we met?'

Buck sensed that this was not a casual question and felt a tension building up between them. He attempted to keep the concern from his face and decided to keep it general. 'Sorta. Kansas way, as I remember? Can't recall exactly where.'

Grant raised his eyebrows. 'What brings you this way?'

'Didn't reckon I'd be known up here. Seems I was wrong.' He wondered where this conversation was going and tried to steer it away from the past. 'Sorry about the circumstances with Frank being killed an' all. You've got a good thing going here. How long have you been operating from this hideaway?'

'We've done OK,' Grant admitted.

'Seems like we're two men down. You aiming to join us?'

'Clint seemed to think so,' Buck said. 'Without him I'd've still been looking at the sky through bars.'

'Yeah,' Grant said. 'Not sure I'd've done the same as Clint, but he can act a mite wild.'

Buck grunted. 'Fact is I'm here now. If I'm not wanted I'll take my leave soon's I've eaten.'

'Not as easy as that,' Grant said, and Buck knew there was an implied threat hidden in those words. 'Ya've gotta prove yerself. Like I hadda do in Six-Mile Canyon. Remember that?'

'Yeah,' Buck said. 'It'd be hard to forget.'

'You and that mad Irishman,' Grant went on, scratching his head. 'What was his name? I promised myself I'd always remember in case I ever met him again.'

'Darned if I can recall it, either,' Buck said, sensing that Grant's questions were entering dangerous ground. 'Don't matter much now, anyway, cos he took a slug in the chest later. Never did take much care of himself.'

Grant nodded in agreement. 'Same as Frank. Didn't know when to duck.'

Buck was grateful for the change of subject. 'Shame the way he got it.'

'Yeah. We're all sorry about Frank, though it was his fault according to what I've bin told, rushing in before checking out the area.'

Buck's peace of mind didn't last long. With a chuckle Grant said, 'An' that time you and me had that fight in the Long Lost saloon. Ya know, I never really thanked you for comin' to my rescue when they pulled a gun on me. Reckon I'd not be here now.'

'You'd've done the same,' Buck said, wondering if Grant was making it all up or if Ray had really done those things. 'Anyway, time I had a look around this place, so mebbe we can talk about old times later.' He turned to walk away, but Grant grabbed his arm.

'I'll show ya,' he said. 'Least I can do after all you did for me.'

Grant guided them away from the huts until they came to an area of broken rocks and scree. 'I nearly met my maker here,' he said. 'These cliffs are dangerous in the rain.' There was a nervous tension in his voice.

They sat on a flat boulder as Grant explained how the gang had accidentally come across this hidden valley and consequently how the men carefully guarded their secret. As he listened Buck was certain that Grant was talking for the sake of talking and that there was something else on his mind.

There was silence for a full minute, each man waiting for the other to speak.

At last Grant turned his gaze on him. 'There's something about you,' he began. 'You and me were close at one time.'

'Uhuh,' Buck said.

With a sudden movement Grant launched himself to his feet, at the same moment snatching his gun from its holster and pointing it at Buck's head.

'What the hell … ?' Buck said, injecting surprise into his voice.

Grant continued to hold the gun steady. 'I don't know who ya are, though ya look mightily like the Ray Norris I used to ride with. But you sure fooled me fer a while.'

'Dunno what you're talking about,' Buck said, rising quickly.

'Show me yer left arm,' Grant snarled.

'What for?'

'Ray took a slug. I won't ask again.'

Buck started to do as he was ordered, knowing that in a few moments he would no longer be able to hide behind his brother's identity.

'Why're you doing this? You know who I am. We're old friends.'

'That mebbe so, but I doubt it. Let's go show the others, see what they make of it.' He gestured for Buck to start walking. 'Seems to me yer playing a dangerous game.'

Buck quickly assessed the situation. He knew that he wouldn't be able to keep up the pretence for long and, once his deception was discovered by these rough-living men, his life expectancy would be very

88

short.

While removing his arm from the sleeve Buck managed to get his hand close to his gun butt.

'You're mistaken,' he said, noticing that Grant had let his gun lower and that he had not yet thumbed back the hammer. This was his only chance and he took it. He drew and brought the barrel up and across, making contact with Grant's head.

Grant fell back without a sound and released his hold on the gun.

'Sorry,' Buck murmured as he bent and examined him for signs of life. Grant was breathing but his head showed a gash that was leaking blood. 'Dammit!' Buck mouthed silently. 'I sure as hell didn't wanna do that.' He sighed inwardly as he fastened his shirt again. 'I've gotta get outta here now for sure.' He picked up Grant's weapon and glanced around to see if anyone had been watching.

So far he was alone. He looked about for a place to hide the wounded man. About thirty feet away was perhaps the perfect place. Buck heaved Grant's body over his shoulder and hurried with it to a large rock fall, half-expecting to be challenged at any moment.

He lowered Grant into a cleft and quickly dragged loose rocks around him. With a quick look around he strolled casually back to where his horse had been tethered and where Clint was clearing away some tall grass.

'Seen Grant anywhere?' Clint asked.

'Spoke to him a while ago,' Buck told him, wondering how he could gather his gear from the bunkhouse without being challenged. 'Said he was going further into the canyon.'

Clint frowned. 'Not like him. Wonder what he's up to.'

Buck shrugged. He had made up his mind to do without his gear when there was a shout. Yol came running and was holding up something in his hand.

'Just found this,' he said, and held out a small piece of silver shaped in the form of a cross with a thin chain. 'This is Grant's. It was lying on the ground. He'd never leave it. Something's happened.'

The commotion had attracted the other members of the gang. 'Has nobody seen Grant?' Growler demanded.

Clint looked at Buck. 'He was OK when he left you?'

'Sure he was.'

Growler gave Buck a long stare. 'We've gotta look fer him afore he wanders too far. Remember what happened last time?'

Buck looked questioningly at Clint.

'He took a slug in his head. It's still there. Doc says it'll kill him one day, but sometimes he fergets where he is.'

'I'll give a hand,' Buck said as the men set off in different directions. But now he seized the chance that had been thrown his way. It took him precious minutes to gather what he needed from the bunk-house, check his saddle, mount up and set his horse at a fast trot.

If he had thought to make his escape without being seen he was disappointed. There was a yell and Growler charged after him. For a large man he moved quickly and Buck set spurs to his mount, racing for the entrance of the hideout.

'Where d'ya reckon yer going?' Growler shouted. 'Come back here!'

Buck ignored the activity behind him and the lead that flew past his head. He lay low over the saddle and urged his mount to more speed. Soon he was out of range, but he had no illusions. He had stirred a hornet's nest and angry men would be chasing him as soon as they had mounted up.

He kept up a fast gallop, then slowed, allowing his horse to maintain a more modest pace that he could keep up for many more miles. He tried to remember the layout of the many canyons that twisted and branched along the way and kept his eyes on a distant escarpment that he thought he recognized.

He frequently looked behind, expecting that he would see signs of those pursuing him. Just when he thought he had evaded pursuit he noticed dust rising from beyond an outcrop on the trail he had taken.

He still kept to a steady pace, knowing and taking confidence in the capability of the animal beneath him. If he kept going long enough to find his way out of the labyrinth he might be able to escape his pursuers and continue on to the next town. Rymansville had outlived its usefulness.

He was relieved when he reached an open area marked by a high pinnacle of rock that he had passed on the way in. Skirting that, he successfully steered his way through several narrow passages until he emerged on to more open terrain and recognized the trail. He set his course towards the east, where he could skirt around the town. He looked back and saw that three of the outlaws were not far behind. He urged his horse to greater effort.

He headed towards a stand of cottonwoods, hoping he would be able to conceal himself there, but as he entered the trees he saw more horsemen coming from the other direction. Surely the outlaws hadn't managed to cut him off?

The riders had not seen him and he was going to keep it that way until he knew who they were. Meantime the out-laws were getting closer.

He reined in while he decided whether to go on, try to turn back or simply stay where he was.

He slid from the saddle and trailed the reins. The gelding calmly cropped the grass that was growing long and sweet underfoot. A small rill ran close by.

There were sudden shouts and shots rang out. He peered from behind his cover and was amazed to see that the two groups of riders were exchanging fire. The outlaws, outnumbered, had turned and raced back towards the high cliffs. The pursuing group chased after them and, now they were closer, Buck recognized the marshal.

'A posse!' He breathed his thanks.

After fifteen minutes, when both he and the gelding had satisfied their thirst, he remounted and set off. He rode slowly, reassured that no one had noticed him. The sound of guns was muffled and getting fainter.

He rode wide of Rymansville but joined

up with the trail he knew well, where he had wounded the rancher's son. That incident had begun Buck's adventure. He vowed never again to go to the aid of a lady in distress.

Thinking of Sam brought her image into his mind, with her long hair, eyes the colour of a summer sky and a mouth that held that ready smile. He allowed himself to dwell on the memory and regretted that he would never see her again.

'Well, well, look who we have here.' A snarling voice, close behind, startled him and caused him to reach for his gun. He whirled. Immediately he knew he was too late, for a six-gun, held in the hand of the young man he had crossed earlier, was levelled at his back. The second youth, who was clearly still in pain from the lead Buck had lodged in his leg, was mounted on another horse. He was grinning broadly.

'I wouldn't advise it,' the young man said. 'That is, if ya wanna live fer a mite longer.'

'What's this about?' Buck queried, although he knew without asking.

'Drop yer gunbelt an' I'll tell ya.'

Buck remained still. 'There's no need for us to fight. Whatever our differences, it's over.'

'It ain't over till I say it is.' He nodded to his companion. 'Jas sorta reckons ya owe him something, so I'll tell you agin fer the last time, shuck yer belt.'

This time, left with no option, Buck obliged and let his gunbelt drop to the ground. 'Dunno what I can offer.'

'Pain!' Jas growed. 'Ya caused me plenty, an' now yer gonna feel some. Git offa yer horse.'

Buck contemplated making a run for it, but he quickly realized that however swiftly his horse could move a bullet travelled faster. He slid from the saddle, eyed the gun lying at his feet and awaited his chance.

9

Baff Finney was very pleased with himself, though he tried not to show it, not in front of the big rancher. Baff had ridden out to the ranch at Walt Grayson's request in the hope that he was going to make a good deal. He hadn't been disappointed.

'So, Walt,' he said. 'Let me get this straight. If I persuade Sam Merryman to sell up to you, ya'll buy my place fer the sum on this here piece of paper. That so?' He gripped the paper tight as his greedy eyes absorbed the figures written there.

Walt Grayson nodded, his face showing no emotion. 'That's the deal. Think you can do it?'

Baff wondered why the rancher, with all his resources, had been unable to settle with Sam Merryman himself. He rubbed the stubble on his chin. 'Easy,' he said. 'Leave it with me.'

The rancher continued as if he hadn't

spoken. 'It'd be a great help to me. I'm a fair man as folk round here know, but I need to expand and Sam's property is standing in my way.'

Baff continued to rub away at his chin. 'What if I can't persuade her? She's a strong-willed bitch.'

'I don't like your language,' Walt growled.

Baff took a step back. 'Sorry, Walt. Didn't mean nothin' by it. Only I could sell ya my place right now.'

Walt shrugged. 'Your place is no good to me without Sam's. If you fail the deal's off. And one more thing.'

'Yeah?'

'Miss Merryman's not to be harmed.'

'Understood,' Baff said quickly. 'I'll go see her this very day.'

The rancher stood, signifying that the meeting was at an end. 'Good, that's settled, then. I'll expect to hear from you within the next twenty-four hours.'

Baff rose also. He left the building, mounted his horse and set off home, a wide grin of satisfaction on his face.

Sam had to come round to his way of thinking. And if she didn't he knew a couple of men who could be persuaded to apply a little pressure. He wondered vaguely why the rancher had not tried that approach to the problem.

There was another little difficulty that Baff had to solve at the same time. His wife, Sarah, held the deeds of the land, and she had made it clear that she did not intend to sell, to Walt Grayson or anyone else.

Baff wondered, not for the first time, how he had let himself get into that position. When he'd married Sarah five years ago he should have insisted then. It just wasn't right for a woman to own property when she had a husband. Sarah and Sam were very similar to each other, ornery, selfish bitches.

But Baff knew how to deal with them both. If Sarah continued to be difficult she might meet with a fatal accident and then the farm would be his. And if Sam refused to sell, well, she might suffer the same fate.

He turned his horse at the junction of the trails and headed out to Sam Merryman's place. He found her forking hay, her arms working rhythmically in easy movements. He watched her for long moments from a distance, admiring the litheness of her body, the flow of her hair as she swung from side to side. Baff had to admit that she was a very desirable woman.

A huge, well-muscled man, known to Baff only as 'Moose', was working nearby and was paying close attention to the visitor. Baff waved his arm to signify his friendly intentions, then pulled his gaze away and urged his horse forward.

Sam looked up as soon as she heard him, laid the fork down and waited for him to approach.

'Hard work for a woman,' Baff observed.

'What is?'

'Running a homestead.'

'No harder than for a man.'

'Sarah was pleased when I came along

to take the heavy work offa her.'

Sam held back a smile. 'The right man can be useful to have around at times.'

'Ever figured on marryin' agin?'

'You don't often come this way, Baff,' Sam said, ignoring his question.

'Reckoned it was time I paid ya a visit,' Baff said with his friendliest smile.

Sam invited him into the house. Baff, acting as he reckoned a gentleman would act, removed his hat and thanked her as he sat and had a steaming mug of coffee placed on the table in front of him.

'We're gonna sell up,' Baff said suddenly.

Sam gazed hard at him. 'Must've been a sudden decision, Baff. I spoke to Sarah in town only two days ago. Seems she was set to stay.'

'Well, she doesn't know it yet,' Baff admitted.

'Then, how … ?'

'Just negotiated a great deal from the rancher. Too good to turn down.'

Sam's curious expression forced him to offer an explanation. 'Yeah, Walt Grayson's prepared to pay generously for the land he wants. Ours and yours,' he added.

'Ah.' Sam breathed deep. 'Baff, I've told Walt and I'm telling you, I'm not selling. So if that's what he or you want you'll both be disappointed.'

Baff's expression changed. He scowled. 'Sarah will sell. So, I reckon, will you.'

Sam stood up. 'What I do or not do is of no concern of yours. I don't know how much Walt has offered you or what you hope to gain from your visit here today, but this is my land and I intend to keep it.'

'You might regret it.'

Sam held her anger in check. 'What I regret, Baff, is giving you the time of day. I think, if you've finished your coffee, you should leave.'

Baff pushed his chair back so hard that it tipped over. He left it where it lay. He strode to the door and wrenched it open.

'Yer gonna sell. I'd advise ya to take Walt's offer afore it's too late.'

Sam held the door open for him. 'Don't be surprised if I don't take your advice.'

He swung round and made a move as if he would strike her. Instead he snarled, 'You'll sell. One way or the other.'

'I don't respond well to threats, Baff,' Sam said. 'Please give my regards to Sarah. And tell her to call in any time.'

'Stupid bitch,' he muttered under his breath.

Baff mounted and rode away without looking back. If he had glanced round he might have noticed that Moose was very close by and, in all probability, had overheard his conversation with Sam.

He rode hard for home. Sarah would be preparing the meal about now. At least, she'd better be because Baff was hungry. Baff was always hungry. For food, women and money. But for now he urgently needed to get ownership of the farm transferred legally to himself. He should have seen to that long ago. He cursed himself again for not having done so.

If he could achieve that quickly he wouldn't have to persuade Sarah to agree to sell. But he decided he could pursue that line of attack anyway.

'Sarah!' he bawled, even before he'd dismounted at the door. 'Sarah!'

His wife appeared, wiping her hands on her apron.

'Where've you been, Baff?'

'Never mind where I've been.' He strode towards her and grasped her by the shoulders, bringing her face close to his. 'We're gonna get this farm into my name, then we're gonna sell up to Walt Grayson. It's a lotta dollars. More'n we'll ever make by stayin' and workin' this miserable piece of land.'

Sarah, clearly taken by surprise by this sudden outburst, tried to pull herself away from his strong grip.

Baff shook her roughly. 'Were ya listenin' to me, woman? I've made up my mind.'

Sarah found her voice. 'I heard what you said, Baff, but this land is mine, just like it was my husband's before he died. We've been through all this before. I'm not selling, no matter how much the rancher's offering.'

Baff struck his wife across the mouth with the back of his hand.

'We're gonna sell! Sam Merryman's agreed. You'll think different when she sells.'

For just a moment Sarah appeared stunned by that possibility. She dabbed at the blood trickling from the corner of her mouth.

'Sam'll never do it!'

Baff cracked a knowing grin. 'Yer wrong.' He had already decided what he was going to do. 'You an' me, we're goin' into town tomorrow to see that clever lawyer. We'll have the deeds transferred. It ain't right fer a woman to keep her husband.'

He slapped her across the side of her head. 'Now git goin' with that chow. We've wasted enough time an' my belly's as empty as a …' His imagination was not up to completing the sentence. 'I'm starving.' He raised his hand again.

But Sarah was away. There was a determination and a confidence in her stride that worried Baff a little, but he soon forgot that as he began to plan. He wasn't without friends who would do anything for a few dollars. After he'd eaten he would pay a visit to the saloon where he was sure he would find them.

10

Buck's opportunity to pick up the gun never came, because the next thing he knew was a sudden blinding pain and blackness as Jas hit him hard on the side of his head.

When he regained consciousness he was lying on the rough ground, tightly bound hand and foot. His head throbbed as he opened his eyes to see the two young men seated on a fallen tree, staring at him with wicked grins distorting their faces.

Buck rolled over and managed to sit up, shuffling to a tree to give support. 'What in tarnation …?' He set his jaw against the pain.

Jas's face hardened. 'Reckon I might've hit ya a mite too hard,' he said. 'You've bin out a whiles. Me an' the Kid here, we're sorta impatient to git on with the show.' He stood, limped across the few yards to where Buck was sitting, drew back his foot and casually kicked Buck in the side. It was a vicious kick. Buck gasped and slipped sideways.

Jas kicked him again, then ground the heel of his boot down on Buck's leg.

'Fight me like a man,' Buck grated. 'There's two of you to one of me. Or are you both too lily-livered to stand up against someone who can hit back?'

This brought more kicks, one of which landed on Buck's face, bringing blood streaming from his nose.

'This ain't no fun,' the Kid said. 'Let's haul him back to the ranch where we kin take our time.' Together they lifted Buck and draped him over his horse's back.

'Best not to fall off,' Jas said. 'Or we'll drag you back.'

The boys were in great spirits as they mounted up and set off along the trail. Buck gritted his teeth, determined not to show his captors how much he hurt. He shut his eyes and tried to conserve his strength while bouts of blackness descended over him.

The sound of a wagon and horses'

hoofs came to him as if in a dream.

'Whoa there,' Jas called, and the wagon stopped.

Buck screwed his head round and managed to get a glimpse of a two-horse wagon, driven by a giant of a man. He heard Jas say, 'Reckon the fun's not over yet. What say we see what he's carryin' in them sacks?'

The Kid said, drawing his gun, 'Git down offa yer wagon, mister, an' step away.'

The giant did so without speaking and stepped across to Buck's side.

'He doesn't look too comfortable,' he observed softly. He lifted Buck from the saddle and let him stand, leaning weakly against the horse's flank.

Buck attempted a smile at the easy manner in which the giant was facing the two men. The man was big by any standards, with deep-set eyes and a well-proportioned muscular frame. Buck also noted that he was not wearing a gun.

'You're Moose, ain't ya?' the Kid asked. 'From that homestead.'

'That's me,' Moose said. 'What can I do for you?'

'We're gonna search yer wagon,' Jas said. 'An' if we find something we want we'll take it and let you go on yer way.'

'Sorry, fellers,' Moose said. 'Can't let ya do that. It all belongs to Miss Merryman. They ain't mine to give you.'

'Don't worry none about that,' Jas sneered. 'It'll all belong to us soon enough. We kin take everything over your dead body if we take a notion to. All I've gotta do is pull this trigger. Now, git over here and take that tarp off so's we kin see what ya got.'

Moose shrugged. 'Don't reckon on dying jus' yet,' he said, and did as he was ordered. 'Help yourselves.'

The Kid climbed up on to the wagon while Jas kept his Colt pointed at Moose, who watched with a slight smile on his face as if he was enjoying the confrontation. His smile became wider when all the Kid found was flour, fat, sugar, corn, pork, vegetables and other supplies. The

110

Kid jumped down.

'We'll have to search you,' he said to Moose. 'Jus' in case yer carrying some money. And don't ferget my pard's got ya covered, so don't try anything funny. Keep yer hands up high.'

Moose again did as ordered and submitted while Jas ran his hands over his body and emptied his pockets.

'Nothin' much there,' Jas said and turned to look questioningly at the Kid. 'What d'ya reckon we do now?'

Moose didn't give them the chance to do anything but grunt as one powerful hand closed around Jas's neck and snapped it. At the same time his other hand swept Jas's gun from its holster and levelled it at the Kid. For a critical moment Moose's body was covered by that of Jas. The Kid's bullet, meant for Moose, struck Jas in the chest. Since Jas was already dead, it didn't matter much. Moose fired and the Kid fell, dead before he hit the ground.

'Dang it!' Moose muttered. 'I didn't wanna do that, but leastwise they didn't feel no pain.' He strolled over to where Buck was trying to remain on his feet. Then, with a knife from his belt he cut the bonds and gently lifted Buck on to the sprung seat of the wagon.

'They do much damage to you?' he asked.

'Nothin' that can't be fixed,' Buck told him, while mopping away the blood that had run down his chin.

'Better get checked over anyway,' Moose said.

Then he assessed the disarray that the Kid had inflicted while raking through the sacks, carefully tidied up the supplies and covered them with the tarp. The two dead bodies he heaved on to the wagon, pulled the tarp over them, tied the spare horses to the rear and climbed up next to Buck.

'They didn't have to die,' he said.

Buck, who was feeling a little stronger, shook his head.

'You had no chance. I owe you, Moose, if that's your name.'

'That's what they call me,' Moose said

and, with a gentle movement of the reins, set the horses in motion.

Buck became suddenly aware that Moose had turned the wagon and was heading back to town.

'Where're we going?' he asked.

'Gotta get you seen to by the doc.'

'Not a good idea,' Buck said. 'I wouldn't be too welcome to the law just now.'

Moose waited for an explanation, but Buck shook his head, although it hurt when he did so.

''Less you know the better, Moose. I'll take my leave of you here. I'm in your debt an' if I can ever repay it I will.' This was the second such promise he'd made. By way of answer Moose turned the wagon again.

'You're not fit to go anywhere. Miss Merryman'll take a look at you. Then I must get these bodies into town. The heat won't do them much good.'

'I had a run-in with them earlier,' Buck said.

'They've been allowed to act wild,' Moose said. 'The youngest sons of the local rancher. They were always causing trouble. Miss Merryman won't be pleased when she sees them. She has enough trouble keeping the rancher at arm's length.'

'There's nothing else you could've done,' Buck repeated.

Moose looked straight ahead and said nothing while Buck relaxed and let the warmth of the sun do its magic on his aching body. He was surprised therefore when the motion of the wagon stopped.

'We're there,' Moose said. 'Come and meet Miss Sam Merryman.'

Moose had pulled up outside a neat, timber-built cabin backing on to a stand of pines. Buck gazed around and was impressed by everything he saw; a small, neat garden surrounded by a white picket fence, and beyond that cows and horses grazing in lush grassland.

As he scrambled painfully down from the wagon Sam emerged from the cabin. They recognized each other immediately.

'What happened to you?' she asked when she noticed his wounds.

'Coupla wild young men took a dislike to me,' he said with a wry smile. 'Same two as chased you.'

She paled. 'I tried to warn you.'

Moose talked to her and pulled back the tarp to show her the two bodies. Her hand flew to her mouth.

'That's the last thing we needed,' she said, but her tone of voice was resigned rather than angry.

'Moose saved my life,' Buck told her.

'Thank you, Moose.' She laid a hand on his arm. 'It was coming to a head anyway.' Without further explanation she ushered Buck inside.

'Let's see what we can do with your injuries.'

Buck followed her while Moose unloaded the supplies before setting off once more.

'What did you mean when you said it was all coming to a head?' he asked.

She busied herself with the preparation of hot water, antiseptic and liniment and began to treat his wounds.

'Since the death of my husband,' she

began, 'I've struggled to maintain this farm. It's good land here, and there's a plentiful supply of water. That's good, but it's also the problem because Walt Grayson is ambitious and is rapidly buying out the local landowners, swallowing up good grazing land. It happens all over the West as the big drives out the small. He's determined to have my land.'

Buck had seen it all before. 'And you don't wanna leave?'

Her eyes blazed. 'My husband built it up. Even if we were being offered double what it's worth I would still refuse to sell.'

Even as she spoke they heard horses approaching the cabin. She peered out through the window and drew in her breath.

'Speak of the devil! Walt Grayson himself. Might as well face him, though.' She opened her door and stood on the step. 'Stay out of sight, please.'

Buck watched as three horsemen reined in their mounts in the yard. The rancher dismounted and strode towards the door with purposeful steps.

116

'We need to speak, Sam' he said.

'We've nothing to talk about, Walt.'

'Oh, but I disagree,' the rancher said.

'Anything you have to say to me you can say right there, but if you've come to ask if I've changed my mind the answer's still the same as it was.'

Walt Grayson's expression didn't change. 'No, I've nothing further to add on that subject, Sam. Far as I'm concerned my offer is reasonable in the circumstances and I hope you will see the wisdom in what I've proposed.

'But there's another matter that's troubling me. One of my sons was injured. Someone put a slug in him while he was riding along with you. I want to know who it was.'

'How should I know? Your sons were chasing me.'

The rancher took another step nearer. 'Don't play games, Sam. If you have the information, which I know you do, I advise you not to withhold it from me.'

Buck had heard enough. He stepped outside and stood next to Sam. For a brief moment there was silence, then Walt's face clouded over, his brows came together and he took another step.

'That's far enough,' Buck said.

'Who're you?'

'Don't much matter who I am,' Buck stated firmly. 'I was being attacked by two young men and I put a bullet in the leg of one of 'em to slow him down. If they told you some other story that's your problem to deal with.'

Buck reckoned that now was not the time to inform the rancher that his two sons were dead and were on their way to the undertaker.

From the corner of his eye he watched the two horsemen, aware that their hands were not far from their guns. He wondered how far the rancher was prepared to go to exact vengeance. Walt Grayson attempted a smile, but it was one tinged with malice.

'Then,' he said, looking directly at Sam, 'my argument is not with you. Please go inside.' He shifted his gaze to Buck. 'Where I come from, shooting someone who is no threat requires retribution, and I intend to ensure that is done.'

Sam remained where she was. 'This is my property, Walt, and there will be no gunplay here.'

Buck saw the slight movement of the rancher's hand and interpreted it as a signal to the two men behind. Before they had time to draw their weapons Buck's Colt was in his hand. He held his gaze on the men as they stared at him angrily. The rancher raised his eyebrows in mock surprise.

'Very impressive, I'm sure, but like Sam has said, there is no need for gunplay here. A proper opportunity will arise later, I feel sure.'

'Then it's time for you to leave,' Buck told him, continuing to hold his Colt steady.

'I shall leave when Sam asks me to,' the rancher said, in an attempt to reassert his hold on the situation. 'And you may lower your gun.'

Buck held it firmly.

'Please go,' Sam said. 'I'm sorry your

son was shot but you really needed to keep them both under control.' She gave a questioning glance at Buck who shook his head slightly.

'I don't need advice on how to look after my own family,' Walt growled, and turning his horse he left, followed by his two gunmen.

Sam watched them go and went back inside the house.

'This isn't your fight,' she said.

Buck shook his head. 'Seems it is. And I don't have to tell you what that man's reaction will be when he learns that his two sons are dead.'

Sam's face went pale. 'I should have told him.'

'He'll learn quickly enough.'

'Then he'll be right back here, looking for you and Moose.'

'I'm sorry,' Buck said. 'I seem to have brought nothing but trouble to your door.'

'You meant well,' Sam said with a smile. 'With Moose's help I can handle most things that come my way. He's as gentle as they come and wouldn't hurt anyone without good cause. But he's also fiercely loyal.'

'Walt Grayson seems to be a very determined opponent.'

Her face softened slightly. 'He won't harm me, but I stand in the way of his ambitious plans. When he learns about his sons I'm afraid he might be out of control.'

Buck considered this. 'Since I've been the cause of all this I figure there's a way I can make it up to you.'

'How? There's nothing anybody can do.'

Buck held her gaze. 'When I was attacked I was on my way out of town. The law's after me as well as a bunch of outlaws. Now I've run foul of the rancher. The best thing would be for me to continue on my way an' to let Walt Grayson believe it was me who killed his sons.'

Sam digested this, but not for long. 'If you want to leave, of course you can, but not on my account. We must tell the story as it was. Keeping to the truth always seemed to me an excellent habit.' She paused in what she was doing. 'Perhaps, while you make up your mind you would explain it all to me?'

Buck told her everything, how he'd met the marshal and been put in jail; how he'd been rescued and then had to escape from the outlaws; and how he had seen Casey Humble and his posse chasing the gang.

'Moose saved my life when he tackled Walt's sons,' he said, and explained the circumstances that led to their death. 'The marshal will know that it was self-defence,' he added. 'But whose side is the law on?'

Sam, who had been listening without interruption, said firmly, 'Not mine.'

'Whose, then?'

'Best ask Casey.'

'I'll forgo that pleasure,' Buck laughed.

'You do seem to have been busy since you arrived.'

'You could say that.'

'Quite a story,' Sam observed. 'So, if I choose not to believe you, I'm in the presence of a dangerous bandit. Am I?'

Buck smiled. 'Neither dangerous nor a bandit. But I seem to have made enemies and I reckon it might put you in danger if I hang around.'

'You're not going anywhere till you've rested,' Sam said.

11

Casey Humble heard the wagon draw up outside his office. His senses, honed during his service as a law officer, told him that it was bringing him trouble. He could deal with trouble, of course, but tonight he was due at a poker game and was just then preparing to make his way to the saloon where his partners would be waiting.

'Dang it!' he muttered as he waited for the inevitable knock on the door and, by habit, kept his hand on the butt of his Colt.

'Ah, Moose,' he said, recognizing his visitor.

'I've brought you two dead bodies, Marshal,' Moose said without waiting for the law officer to say anything further.

Casey drew in his breath. 'Two dead bodies, huh. Where'd ya happen to find them?'

'I killed them,' Moose said.

Casey shifted in his chair. 'How'd ya manage to do that?'

'One's got a broken neck. The other's got lead in him.'

'Have I got this right, Moose? You broke a man's neck? Then ya shot the other one?'

'Yep, Marshal. I hadda do something, but his neck broke easy, an' then he was shot by the other man, though he was dead by that time, and I hadda shoot back.'

The marshal stroked his whiskers, a habit he had acquired whenever he was perplexed. 'Yer not makin' sense, Moose. Who are these men?'

'The rancher's sons,' Moose said without emotion, but his words had a severe effect.

'You killed Walt Grayson's sons!'

'Well, it weren't exactly like that, Marshal. Like I said, they were intent on harming someone an' I hadda stop them or they were gonna kill him. Me, too, I reckon.'

Casey Humble pushed himself out of the comfort of his chair.

'The rancher's sons!' he repeated, as if he couldn't believe what he was being told. 'Let's see what ya got.' He led the way outside and lifted the corner of the tarp, revealing the bodies beneath. He remained staring at them for some time before covering them up again.

Several folk had gathered, sensing that Moose had brought in something interesting. Casey studied them and beckoned someone over.

'Go fetch the undertaker for me. Tell him it's urgent.' He turned to Moose. 'Come inside, I wanna go over ya story again.'

Moose sat and talked, with the marshal asking questions.

'Who was the man you rescued, Moose?'

'Never met him before. Said his name was Buck. He was badly hurt. I offered to bring him in to see the doc. He didn't want that so I took him out to the homestead. Miss Merryman seemed to know him.'

The marshal pondered this information. The situation was getting more serious by the minute.

'He's a dangerous man,' he said. 'Miss Merryman may be putting herself in harm's way by taking him in.'

Moose stood up. 'I'd better get back, then,' he said.

'Whoa! Just a minute.' Casey also rose to his feet and came round the desk fast. 'I can't let ya go just like that, Moose. It's not just that there's two dead men out there, it's that they're the sons of Walt Grayson. That makes a difference. A big difference. An' you've admitted to killin' them. Unless you kin produce a witness showing it was self-defence I have to treat it as murder. You know how it is, Moose.'

'Miss Merryman needs me back at the homestead,' Moose stated simply. 'I ain't going into no jail.'

'Sorry, Moose. I'll take a trip out to Sam's an' let her know the situation. Your life won't be worth a dime when Walt Grayson hears about this.' He raised his

Colt. 'I hope you're not gonna be difficult, Moose. I'll let ya go if the man you saved confirms your story.

'Now, walk in front of me through that door. Nice an' easy. Don't make me have to use this.' He motioned with the gun. 'I'll let Sam know soon's I can.'

Moose obeyed slowly and he was soon inside the cell that Buck had recently occupied. He gripped the bars and Casey wondered for a moment whether this giant of a man had the strength to bend them.

The sun had been gone for an hour when Buck awoke from a light sleep. He stretched and yawned and eased his aching muscles where the young man's boots had inflicted damage. After some soup and a mug of fresh coffee, served up by Sam, he felt better.

'Moose hasn't returned,' Sam said suddenly.

Buck cupped his hands around the warm mug. 'Is that unusual?'

'He never stays away,' she said. 'Doesn't

128

go into the saloon. He should have been back by now. I'm worried.'

Buck heaved himself to his feet. 'I'll take a ride into town. Any special place I should be looking?'

'You can't do that,' Sam said. 'Not after what you told me. You'll be arrested.'

Buck strapped on his gunbelt and took his Stetson down from the peg. 'Least I can do. I'll keep outta trouble.'

'If you must go you could try the livery. All the stores will be closed, although you may find Maisie's eating house still doing business. Moose and Maisie like each other, but even so ...' Her voice trailed off.

'Sounds a likely place to try first.' He strode out through the door, eager to repay some of the kindness he had received from this remarkable woman.

As he set his horse towards town he wondered what he might be riding into. He still had to look out for Clint and his outlaws, who might be hunting for him. The rancher's hired guns would also be on his trail with murder on their minds. And he could hardly ask for the protection of the law in the form of Casey Humble after the humiliation that had been heaped upon him.

The moon was bright enough to give him a clear view of the trail ahead, and he remained alert for the slightest signs of danger. By the time he had reached the outskirts of the town he had met no one and seen no one, and his approach didn't seem to arouse much interest.

There was no sign of Moose at either of the places Sam had mentioned, but the information he received from Maisie herself set him wondering.

'Moose called in on his way to the law office,' she told Buck, concern in her voice. 'He said he'd be back to see me, but he never showed up so I went down to speak to Casey Humble.'

She took a deep breath. 'Moose has been locked up! I asked Casey why and he told me it was none of my business. Wouldn't even let me talk to him.'

Buck thanked her and made his way slowly to the marshal's office. He was in no doubt what sort of welcome he would receive, but it was possible that by now the lawman might have realized his mistake.

And if that wasn't likely Buck had some information about Clint's outlaw gang that he would be able to provide. It was probable, however, that the posse that Casey had been leading had already succeeded in killing the outlaws or had put them behind bars. In which case his bargaining chips were very few.

He hitched his horse outside the law office, climbed the three steps to the boardwalk and rapped at the door. He pushed it open without waiting for a reply, stepped inside and kept his hands high. At his appearance Casey Humble leaped to his feet, gun in hand. A mug of coffee tipped over and spilled its contents on to the wooden desk.

'Hell!' The marshal gave a stunned grunt.

'Yeah,' Buck drawled. 'Reckoned it's time for us to be better acquainted.'

Casey's eyes glared at him. 'Hand over yer gun an' I might be more inclined to listen to ya.' He mopped up the spilled liquid. Buck slid the Colt from its holster and held it out, butt first.

'Sorta yours in the first place if I recall. Mine's still at the saloon, but I hadda leave in a hurry.'

'Now siddown, an' don't get any ideas. I'll shoot at the first sign.'

'I'm here to talk, Marshal.'

'Last time I saw you I was tied up like a hog. I didn't take friendly to that an' it's not gonna happen again.'

'Sorry about that, Marshal, but you were aiming to hang me.'

'Still am,' Casey growled. 'Let's git the yapping over so's I kin lock you up.'

'Ya've got a prisoner in your cells. Moose is the name I know him by. He works for Sam Merryman out at —'

'I know damn well who he works for, an' I'm sorry fer havin' to arrest him, but he killed two young men, the sons of Walt Grayson. Said it was self-defence. Said you were a witness.'

'That what he told you?'

'Yep.'

'There's more to it than that, Marshal. Yeah, I saw exactly what happened. Fact is I wasn't in a position to do anything about it.'

The marshal listened while Buck related the events leading up to the killings.

'He had no choice, Marshal. If he hadn't done what he did I reckon you'd be burying me in boot hill right now.'

'Woulda saved me a job,' Casey said. The corners of his mouth twitched and it seemed to Buck that the marshal was enjoying this. 'So, you're saying you're a witness an' on your say-so I should let him go.'

'That's what I'm saying.'

'You know who those two bucks were?'

'Yeah.'

'Then you'll know what's gonna happen soon as Walt Grayson gits to hear of it?'

'Depends.'

The marshal furrowed his brow. 'Depends on what?'

Buck hesitated. 'Whether the rancher calls the tune around here.'

'He near as hell owns the town.'

'And the law?'

This time the marshal's face turned red with anger. 'Yer saying I'm in his pay?'

'Are you?'

'That's enough! We've finished talkin', so stand up an' git to the cells. I reckon you know the way.'

'And Moose?'

'He stays where he is.'

'You still b'lieve I'm Ray Norris?'

Casey twisted his mouth. 'I do, till proven otherwise.' He stood and gestured with the gun.

Buck rose to his feet, disappointed that his gamble had failed.

12

Neither man had time to move before the office door was thrust open with such force that one of the hinges gave way. Walt Grayson marched into the office and planted himself in front of the marshal, feet apart, eyes fixed on the law officer.

'My sons! My sons've been killed, shot down without a chance to defend themselves. What've you done about it?'

Casey Humble stood his ground. 'I'm sorry 'bout yer sons, Walt. Really am, but —' he began. The rancher cut him short.

'You're not half as sorry as the man who gunned them down'll be. Who was it?'

'I'm investigating,' Casey said.

'Investigating? What's that s'posed to mean? I hear you've got someone locked up already.' He seemed to notice Buck for the first time. 'What've you got to do with this?'

Buck glanced at the marshal, who nodded as if to give permission for him to go ahead.

'Your two sons,' Buck began, keeping his voice level, 'bushwhacked me on the trail outta town. They tied me up an' beat me an' were talking about taking me somewhere so's they could damage me some more. I reckon I'm lucky to still be alive.'

'Why the hell would they do that?'

Buck held the rancher's gaze. 'On account I put a slug in Jas's leg earlier.'

'Did you kill my sons?'

'I told you, I shot him to take his mind off shooting me. I didn't kill your sons, but I reckon they had that in mind for me.'

'They must've had good reason.'

Buck left that remark unanswered. The rancher transferred his attention to Casey.

'Sounds like you're failing in your duties, Marshal. My two sons are dead all on account of this man here, and there you were yapping with him like an old friend. Why isn't he locked up? I want justice, and by God I'll get it.'

'You can safely leave it to the law,' Casey said, a sharpness entering his tone.

'I am the law!'

'But I'm wearin' the star.'

Walt Grayson drew his lips back in a snarl. 'Report to me in the morning. I expect results or you'll be looking for another job.' With that he strode out of the office.

Casey sighed and sank back in his chair, gesturing for Buck to do the same. The marshal poured out two fresh mugs of coffee from the stove and pushed one across the desk.

'Thanks, Marshal,' Buck said and drank the contents gratefully. 'I had a run-in with the rancher earlier at Miss Merryman's place. Does he really own this town?'

'He certainly thinks so,' Casey said wearily.

'Does he own you?' Buck reckoned he knew the answer to that.

'He don't pay my wages,' Casey said

137

after a long pause. He seemed to pull himself together. He thumbed towards the cells. 'If Walt Grayson learns the truth Moose's life won't be worth a bent dime. Don't reckon yours is worth much, neither.'

Buck nodded. 'If Moose ever gets to trial I'll be witness.'

'If either of you live that long. An' it's my job to see that you do.'

'How're ya gonna do that, Marshal?'

'I'm gonna put you in the cells.' Casey grinned. 'Safest place fer you to be till I've figured how to play this.'

'I can look after myself, Marshal.'

'Mebbe. Mebbe not.' He raised his voice towards the cells. 'Moose, c'm 'ere!'

Buck watched in surprise as Moose appeared.

'Saw no need to lock the door,' Casey said. 'Did you hear all that, Moose?'

'I was listening,' Moose said. 'I reckon I should go tell the rancher how it was.'

'Only if ya wanna die young,' Casey said. He gazed at Buck. 'You came into my town unknown. Best if you leave the same way.'

'Thought you were gonna lock me up.'

'Still holding on to that idea.'

'Seems like I started something when I arrived. Least I can do is to see it through.'

'Not if you're behind bars!'

'I like that word, 'if', Marshal. I reckon you had me down as a dangerous outlaw. What's changed your mind?'

Casey scratched his head. 'Danged if I know. Mebbe I haven't.'

Buck laughed, perhaps for the first time since he had set foot in Rymansville.

'Here's something to help you make up your mind. Shoulda told you before.'

He related how, after he had been broken out of jail, Clint had taken him to the hideout of the outlaw gang.

'Really am sorry I hadda leave you tied up, Marshal, but you might've had ideas about stopping me.'

'You drank my whiskey,' Casey grumbled.

'Yeah, but it seemed a waste to leave it on account of you couldn't get to it yourself.'

'Yeah, I can see how that might've coloured your judgement.'

'Who untied you?'

'I didn't stay hogtied fer long. Those varmints were set on robbin' our bank. Soon's you were gone my deputy came to tell me the bank was bein' held up. That's not something we appreciate very much in this town. You can imagine I was all fired up. Lead had started to fly and we got 'em holed up, killed one, but hadda let the others go. Took me as a hostage.'

'It was all planned,' Buck said. 'Rescuing me and robbing the bank at the same time. Didn't quite work out the way they wanted.'

'Got a posse together at sunup, followed their trail, though I didn't hold out much hope of findin' them. Then we saw three of 'em riding out from the rocks. Thought I recognized one of 'em.'

'I can give you a name for most of them,' Buck said.

'They turned tail soon as they saw us, an' we gave chase.'

'I watched you for a while,' Buck said. 'But I couldn't hang around too long.'

'Well, we didn't have much luck. They disappeared in that maze of canyons.'

'Nearly got lost in there myself.'

'Yep, they disappeared.' Casey started to grin. 'All except one. Clint's horse stumbled an' we were on him.'

'Clint?'

'Yeah. He's behind bars back there. Wanna go an' see?'

Buck rose slowly and made his way towards the cells.

'You!' Clint grated. 'You bin with the law all along.'

'Yeah, me,' Buck agreed.

'Ya come to git me out? Ya owe me.'

'Sorry, Clint. Can't do that.'

Clint bared his teeth. 'You're a dead man.'

'Not the first time someone told me that,' Buck said. 'But, yeah, I owe you.'

'Better watch yer back.'

'Hope I didn't hit Grant too hard.'

'Mebbe yer should have.'

'I'll do what I can for you,' Buck said.

141

'But the marshal's more'n a mite sore at being tied up in his own office.'

Buck left Clint mumbling to himself and returned to the office.

'So, I'm free to go?'

'Yep,' Casey told him. 'An' Moose is going back to the homestead. Says Sam can't manage without him.'

'Why're you letting us go, Marshal?' Buck asked. 'It ain't that I don't appreciate it.'

'My business,' Casey told him curtly. 'Save me a loada trouble that way. I don't expect to see either of you again. Anyway, I can find Moose any time. As fer you, I figure you might be who you say you are.'

'I'm not aiming to go anywhere,' Buck said. 'I reckon to hang around for a while, see how things pan out.'

The marshal grinned. 'I figured as much, but that's not what I was thinking.'

'What were you thinking? I ain't running.'

'Truth is, I didn't reckon you'd be leaving, that mebbe you've got more'n a passing interest here.'

Buck reckoned so too, but he said nothing.

Casey let the silence lengthen. He grinned again. 'A man can often find a powerful reason to stick around. Can't say as I blame you.'

Buck ignored the innuendo. 'Told you. I ain't goin' anywhere.'

Casey became serious. 'Soon as Walt Grayson figures out who killed his sons Moose's life won't be worth much. Yours neither. An' you've got the rest of Clint's outlaw gang to reckon with.'

'Best come back with me,' Moose said. 'You can bunk in with me.'

'Barn'll suit me,' Buck told him. 'Slept in worse places than that.'

'Best watch your backs an' sleep with one eye open. Mebbe both,' Casey said, as Buck and Moose left the office together.

'Thanks for the advice, Marshal,' Buck called over his shoulder. 'An' the coffee.'

13

The marshal sat for a few minutes after they had gone while he worked out what he was going to do. He wasn't sure he had done the right thing in letting either Moose or Buck leave. It was likely that there would be two more dead bodies to bury before the sun rose again.

Did it matter? That wasn't the question he should have been asking, but he didn't know what the right question was.

At length he stood up slowly and left the office, pulling the door to behind him. It hung on one hinge. There was only a short walk to the saloon where he knew he would find who he was looking for. They would be in a private room at the back, playing serious cards.

He pushed through the batwings and strode up to the bar. A quick whiskey would fortify him before he announced the bad news. He emptied the glass in one swallow, nodded to the barkeep and went through a door marked private.

He entered the smoke-filled room without knocking. Samuel Sniper looked up with annoyance.

'What is it, Casey?'

'We need to talk,' Casey said.

'Can't it wait? We're in the middle of a game.'

The marshal glanced at the heaped-up pile of dollar notes.

'Sorry, Samuel, but it's kinda important.' He stepped away from the table and stood patiently until the hand had been played. Samuel Sniper slammed his cards down and pushed himself to his feet.

He and the three other men, James Marley, Ben Purdy and Milo Miles, levelled their gaze at the lawman.

'What is it, Marshal?' Oswald demanded. 'Better be something really important. We pay you to handle things.'

'Yeah,' Casey said. 'And so far I've kept this town law-abiding.'

'But not too law-abiding,' James said with a smirk.

'Business doin' well?' Casey asked.

Oswald let out a roar of satisfaction. 'Couldn't be better. S'far as I'm concerned you've done a great job.'

Ben Purdy nodded his head in agreement. 'Sales goin' at a great pace,' he chortled. Casey knew what they were telling him. Lawlessness brought trouble, but with trouble came big profits for those in a position to take advantage. Peaceful days and wild nights was the creed these businessmen went by.

'What progress,' Milo Miles asked in a voice that conveyed his dissatisfaction, 'have you made since my bank was attacked?'

'We shot one and caught another,' Casey said. 'He's now in jail. We also know where they've bin holed up, but I reckon they won't be using that place any more.' He swept his gaze over the three men. 'But somethin' more serious has come up.'

'There's nothing more serious than my bank being robbed.'

Casey did not feel overawed in the least

146

by any of these gentlemen. He considered them pompous and self-interested. He knew, as most other folk did, that they were in the pockets of Walt Grayson.

'Yeah this matter is more serious. And your bank wasn't robbed.'

'Damn near it, though.' The banker thumped the table, causing whiskey to spill.

' 'Damn near' ain't what I'd call 'actual'.'

Oswald Marley grunted in annoyance. 'Enough of that! What've you got to tell us?'

Casey drew in a breath. 'A short time ago two dead bodies were brought into town an' are now with the undertaker.' He paused. 'The dead men were two sons of Walt Grayson.'

There were four collective gasps.

'How'd they die?' Ben Purdy asked.

'Shot.'

The questions came quickly.

'D'you know who shot them?'

'Does the rancher know?'

'What're you doing about it?'

Casey nodded. 'Yeah, I know how it happened and yeah, Walt Grayson knows about it an' is looking for someone to lynch.' He went on to explain what Moose had told him.

'And Moose is locked up?'

'There was a witness confirmed Moose's story.'

'Who?'

'Drifter by the name of Buck. The same the boys were threatening to kill.'

'An' you believe him?'

'Yep.'

The four men conferred. The chairman turned.

'We can't allow Walt Grayson to take the law into his own hands, so we, you, must have somebody in custody, arrange a quick trial and a legal hanging. We pay you and expect you to do a good job. See to it.'

Casey took a deep breath.

'Two things wrong with that. First, you don't pay me. The town pays me an' the rancher bankrolls the town. Second, the only suspect is Moose an' no judge is gonna convict him on account of he has a witness to the fact that it was self-defence.'

'Then,' Samuel drawled, 'you'll have to discredit the witness. Go to it, Casey. Report back to us by noon tomorrow. The last thing we want is for Walt Grayson to withdraw his support for this town.'

Casey understood that the town council, as represented by the four men, would not be looking for justice, but for results that would make the problem go away. As things stood they were up to their armpits in dollars. Anything that interrupted the flow was to be avoided.

He rose from the table. 'I'll do what I can,' he said, nodded and left.

It seemed that he would not be taking part in the game he had been looking forward to tonight.

Late as it was he went back to his office and sat awhile, going over in his mind the conversation he had just had with those worthies of the town. Perhaps he'd played their game long enough. Was it time to show them that he could not be pushed around any longer?

Then it occurred to him that he had not yet done his evening rounds. He rose wearily.

The moon showed itself only briefly as Buck and Moose rode out of town together. They felt safer in the dark, knowing that there was less chance of being shot in the back. Nevertheless, they kept alert, watching for movement and listening to any sounds that would warn them of danger.

At first Moose showed no inclination to talk and Buck was content to ride in silence, absorbed in his own thoughts. Without intending to he had stirred up a rattler's nest, put lives in danger and brought to a head something that had been simmering under the surface.

They'd been going for thirty minutes when Buck said, 'Sorry, Moose.' He said it almost to himself but Moose heard.

'Ain't nothing to be sorry fer,' Moose said.

'You saved me from a beating. Probably

saved my life and all I've done for you is to put you in bad with the law an' make things worse for Sam.'

Moose turned in the saddle. 'Miss Merryman knew Walt Grayson wouldn't hold off for ever. He's been wanting to marry her and she's strung him along, but he's not a patient man. He's determined to win her and the homestead for himself. Soon's he's sure he can't get it legally he won't hold back.'

'What about the law?' Buck asked.

'Casey Humble's been too long in the job. He does what he's told to do, though I reckon I've seen a change in him.'

'He's given me fair treatment considering,' Buck said. They were nearing the homestead when he suddenly reined in his horse. He sat and listened.

'What's that noise?'

Moose pulled up. 'Voices,' he said. 'Men! Miss Merryman's!'

Then they heard the gunshot and urged their horses into speed. As they breasted the last hill they saw the glow of a fire where a barn had been set alight.

Silhouetted against the flames were two riders, seemingly intent on spreading the fire rather than containing it.

Without further thought Buck set his mount down the slope at full speed. Moose was only a few yards behind him. Buck withdrew his rifle from its scabbard and tossed it to Moose.

'Ya might be needin' this.' He drew his Colt and fired some shots into the air.

At the same time a flash came from one of the cabin's windows and the deeper sound of a rifle added to the din.

Closer still, Buck slowed and aimed deliberately at the figures on horseback. Moose, firing the rifle, kept going fast, shouting as he went.

The two men whirled to meet this new threat and fired blindly into the gloom. One of them clutched his chest and slid into the dirt. His horse, taking fright, ran off some fifty yards. The other man, sensing that the time had come for a quick retreat, whipped his horse around and made for the thin stand of trees outlined against the sky.

At the same time Buck, glancing towards the house, was relieved to see Sam run out of the door with her rifle held ready for use.

'Go after him!' Moose called, pointing to the fleeing man. 'I'll check on the fire.'

With a quick glance at the remains of the barn, Buck yelled at Moose, 'I'll get the goddamn varmint.'

He didn't wait for acknowledgement, but from the corner of his eye he saw that Moose had swerved away towards the house. Then all his attention was on the fleeing horseman. But almost immediately he lost sight of him.

He approached the trees at full speed. He angled slightly so that if someone was lying in wait for him he would not present such an easy target, travelling as he would be side-on to their line of fire.

But no shots met him as he skirted the trees, searching for his quarry. He rode hard for another fifty yards, then reined in, quickly slid from the saddle and listened. He heard it, the sound of a horse thrashing through the undergrowth, its rider invisible in the darkness under the trees.

Buck remounted and, instead of entering the trees, circled around them, hoping to catch his man emerging from shelter. He stopped and listened for a second time.

There was silence.

The clouds cleared, allowing the light from the moon to bathe the ground in an eerie glow. Buck knew that he was clearly at a disadvantage out in the open, while his quarry was concealed in the trees. He moved on, lying low in the saddle, waiting and listening, but he heard nothing.

He considered his options. Without knowing exactly where the man was hiding Buck reckoned that it would have been foolhardy to go in after him. And he didn't fancy sitting his horse in the hope that the man would give himself away.

There was still the man lying on the ground back by the barn. At least identifying him would give a lead as to who had been responsible for the attack.

As Buck turned to go back to the scene

of the fire to examine the dead man a six-gun cracked and lead whistled past his ear. He had seen the flash and immediately fired at the exact spot, then to the left and then to the right of it. There was no answering shot.

As he searched the trees he heard another pistol shot but this time it was muffled. It was followed by the crack of a rifle, both shots coming from the other side of the trees.

Buck dug his heels in and circled the trees once more.

'It's me,' he yelled in case Sam or Moose might have been tempted to put a shot his way. He reined in sharply in front of Moose.

'What's going on?'

'He came back fer his pard, but he didn't get that far. Sam took a shot an' might've winged him, but he high-tailed outta there quicker than he came in.'

The barn had burned to the ground, smouldering embers being all that was left of it. The building had been isolated from the rest of the structures, and it seemed that the men who had lit the fire had done so as a warning. While there was still the danger that sparks could be carried by the light breeze, Buck was pleased to see that Moose had doused the glowing timbers. Moose nodded towards the house.

'Can't do no more here. Let's get a closer look at that varmint, see if we can tell where he came from.'

'I guess we can have a pretty good idea,' Buck suggested.

He slipped from the saddle and, with a last look round, tethered his horse and walked beside Moose towards the body.

'He's still alive!' he said as the man shifted and let out a groan. They saw his chest rise and fall in fast, shallow breaths.

They approached him carefully, Buck covering him with his gun. Moose bent and quickly slipped the man's Colt from the hand that was still grasping it. He placed it in his own waistband.

'Best take him inside,' Buck said.

Moose hoisted up the man easily and carried him gently like a sleeping baby.

'He's still bleeding,' he said. 'Looks

156

bad.'

The man groaned again several times as if to prove it as they walked towards the house.

'Hope he's fit enough to tell us something,' Moose said. 'Mebbe the doc kin patch him up enough to talk.'

Buck, who was a few steps behind Moose, yelled, 'He's got a knife!'

Moose had already felt the movement and his hand shot down, gripped the man's wrist and twisted hard, snapping the bone. The man uttered a final groan and went limp.

'Thanks, Buck,' Moose said, looking decidedly embarrassed. 'I should've bin ready fer that.'

Inside the house they lay the man on the floor and examined him. Blood stained his shirt where the bullet had struck. He was alive but close to death, his bewhiskered face white and bloodless. Sam placed a pillow under his head.

'No reason why we shouldn't make him comfortable,' she said. She held a pad over his wound. Buck knelt down beside the dying man.

'What's yer name?'

'Greg.' It was no more than a whisper.

'You're dying, you sonofabitch. The least you can do is tell us who you're working for.'

There was no answer.

'Who d'you take orders from? Is it Walt Grayson?'

The man coughed. 'Never heard of him,' he spat.

There was a further prolonged bout of coughing and Greg's head fell back. He exhaled for the last time.

Buck felt for his pulse, looked up at the others and shook his head.

'Ever seen him before?' he asked. Sam and Moose shook their heads.

'Thought I might've recognized the other one, but in the dark I couldn't be sure,' Moose said. 'Anyway, we know who sent them.'

'I'm not so sure,' Sam said. 'I don't believe Walt would do that.'

'Who else, then?' Moose asked.

Buck gnawed his lower lip. 'I'm having

trouble gettin' a slant on all this. If not the rancher, then who? Walt Grayson seems like he can do anything he wants so he sends in a coupla men to put a scare into you.

'And where does the marshal stand when folk like Sam are being driven out? Whose pay is he taking? Why did he let us go? There's a load of questions I need answers to. An' I'm gonna get them.

'First thing is to get this body outta the house an' covered up ready to take into town at sunup.'

Moose led the way outside, carrying the body. They took it to another barn, close to the house.

'If they'd set this one alight it would've been another story,' Buck said.

Moose was silent and Buck suspected he was blaming himself for not being there when the attack came.

'Well, we've still got the dead man's horse,' Buck continued. 'That should tell us what we want to know.'

They approached the animal carefully. As they examined its brand it pricked up its ears and flared its nostrils.

'Whose brand is it?' Buck asked.

'Don't know that one,' Moose admitted. 'We'll ask Sam what she wants us to do.'

'I know what I'm going do,' Buck grated. 'I'm going to pay a visit to Walt Grayson, ask if he sent his men to torch Sam's place.'

'This ain't your fight,' Moose said. 'An' it ain't your decision. Might be that Sam don't wanna do anything about it.'

Buck shrugged. What Moose said was true. Perhaps he should mind his own business. He held that view only until he and Moose were seated in the room that served as a kitchen, while Sam, not yet recovered from her scare, was serving them coffee.

'I've had enough of living in fear,' she admitted. 'I think the time has come for me to accept Walt Grayson's offer. If he wants my place so badly he'd better have it.'

'I don't think that's a good idea,' Buck said quietly.

Sam rounded on him. 'I didn't ask for your opinion,' she said, and immediately threw her hand up to her mouth. 'Oh, sorry, I didn't mean that as it came out. What I meant to say was that you needn't be involved any more. I've put up with Walt's advances for a long time and I've told him I won't marry him under any conditions. This was his answer.'

'From the damage his men did he wasn't intending to burn you out,' Buck suggested.

Sam's face hardened. 'If he thinks this is the way to win my heart he's very much mistaken. But I've had enough.' She looked apologetic. 'I'm sorry, Moose. You've been so good to me, taking care of everything, working like two men.' She reached up and laid her hands on Moose's shoulders.

Moose's face flushed. 'You and ya husband treated me well when ya found me half dead,' he said. 'We could still work this place.'

Sam grimaced. 'There's nothing left for us here. I've got to face the fact that if Walt Grayson wanted he could burn us out and I'd have to leave with nothing. If I sell to him at least I'll have something so that I can start up again somewhere else. Perhaps I should marry him, after all. That would be the sensible thing to do.'

Buck somehow found that idea unsettling. 'Sensible perhaps, but giving yourself to a bullying, avaricious man is not the recipe for a happy future.'

'What else can I do? I can't fight someone like him.'

Buck was thoughtful. 'No,' he said slowly. 'But I can.'

'Why should you take on my problems?'

Buck could have suggested an answer to that, but didn't.

'Don't forget I got involved when I wounded one of his sons. The fact that those two sons are now dead is something Walt Grayson won't forget or forgive.

'He'll know by now that Moose killed at least one of them an' he won't let that rest. That was on account of me, an' I owe Moose my life. I'm in your debt, too.

162

Seems to me that Walt Grayson has had everything his own way for too long.'

'Don't do anything that's going to get you killed,' Sam said. 'You might owe Moose, but you owe me nothing.'

Moose interrupted. 'I got a say in this. I'm with Buck. Mebbe between us we might make Walt Grayson think again.'

Buck smiled. 'Thanks, Moose. Reckon first off, afore we do anything, I'll have a word with the marshal. I'm not sure which side he's on, but I reckon he might be comin' round to our way of thinking.'

Sam, who was gazing out of the window, said, 'You won't need to go far.'

Buck looked up questioningly.

Sam pointed. 'Casey Humble's just entered the yard.'

'Wonder what he wants,' Buck mused. 'If he's gonna arrest me agin he'll find I ain't goin' so easy this time.'

14

Making an arrest did not seem to be the marshal's intention. As he dismounted he gazed at the remains of the fire.

'What the hell happened here?'

'Nothing we can't handle, thanks, Casey,' Sam said.

'That's not what I asked, but if you don't wanna tell me that's OK by me. I've got enough problems brewing to keep me busy.'

Sam invited him into the house. 'Sorry, Casey,' she said. 'I'm a bit shaken up. You'll hear about it soon enough, I guess. A visit from two men who took a dislike to my barn.'

'Did you recognize them?'

'One's dead. The other left for the good of his soul,' Buck said.

The marshal sucked in his breath. 'Dead, ya say? Seems to me there's bin a whole lot of dead bodies just lately.

Where've you put him?'

The men made their way to the barn and drew back the tarp.

'Yeah, seen him around,' Casey breathed. 'Drinks with the rancher's men sometimes, but I don't reckon he was regular employed there. Had occasion to haul him in, but nothin' serious. Can't say as how anyone'll mourn his passing.'

'We figured that out already,' Buck said.

The marshal directed his gaze at Buck and Moose. 'What was your part in this?'

'We saw the fire,' Buck said. 'Took some shots at the varmints. Got this one. The other's probably toting some lead that he didn't want. Last we saw of him he was high-tailing that way.' He gestured.

'I reckon the Grayson ranch is kinda in that direction,' Casey mused. 'Let's git back inside. I feel sorta vulnerable out here.'

While they had been gone Sam had been heating some beef stew, and the aroma met the men as they entered.

'That smells real good,' Casey said.

'Perhaps you'd like to try some, then,' Sam said with a smile.

Casey grinned back. 'I'd sure like that. Any of you hurt?' He looked at Sam, who shook her head. 'I'd sure like to keep it that way.'

'Reckon there's been trouble ever since I set foot in this town,' Buck said.

'I can't deny you've stirred things up a bit.'

'Didn't reckon to.'

'Not a bad thing, though.' Casey sat at the table and wiped his hands down his pants before reaching out for a hunk of bread. 'My jail's bin under-used. You were my first customer for months.'

'Couldn't complain about the service,' Buck said. Casey laughed, a good-humoured, full-blooded roar.

'The town council don't 'preciate it if I arrest folk. They make more money when there's a ruckus, 'specially as Walt Grayson bankrolls any losses.'

'Don't seem much need for a lawman,' Buck observed.

'That's about to change.' Casey

tightened his lips. 'I'm gonna do the job I'm paid for, town council or no town council. I've had a run-in with those worthy gentlemen an' I reckon they're just about now deciding how to get rid of their pesky lawman.'

Sam served them all with a good helping of steaming food from the pot.

'Walt Grayson's the man who runs things around here,' she said. 'He wants this land. He scared off my hired help last year so there's only Moose and me left to run this place. His sons were allowed to harass me. And now he's sending his men to set fire to my property.'

'That's still to be proved, Sam,' Buck told her, cautiously.

'He'll deny it.'

Casey straightened his shoulders. 'I'll prove it or find the men responsible.'

'You can't fight him, Casey. He's got the town buttoned up.'

'Right,' Casey said as he mopped up the last of the stew from the plate with a final hunk of bread. 'We'll see about that. Glad to find ya all at home.' He drained his coffee and took a cheroot from his vest pocket. 'D'you mind if I light up, ma'am?'

Sam smiled with pleasure. 'My husband used to smoke those things, Casey. I've missed the smell since he went.'

The lawman took his time to get the cigar going to his satisfaction. The others waited for him to go on.

'I've no wish to quit my job without a fight. I reckoned it was time to find out who I could call on to back me up if it comes to that.'

Buck asked, 'D'you still b'lieve I'm an outlaw?'

'Nope.'

'Then I've got nothin' to lose by comin' in with you.'

'D'ya b'lieve I murdered those two sons of Walt Grayson?' Moose asked.

'Nope. Self-defence. No doubt about it.'

'Then, for what it's worth, you can rely on me.'

'You know you can rely on me, too, Casey,' Sam said. 'But I don't know what I can do to help. Looks like I shall have to give up this homestead and move on.'

Buck rapped on the table. 'Not yet you won't. Not now. Not ever. 'Less you want to.'

The marshal directed his law-keeper's gaze at him.

'Not intendin' to break the law, are you?'

'Dunno how you could even ask such a question,' Buck grinned. 'Naw, just before you turned up I'd made up my mind to pay a visit to our big rancher. Talkin's good. Mebbe we'll find out what he really wants.'

'Don't recommend that,' Casey said.

'Wouldn't expect you to.'

'You'll be walkin' into a bear's den. Walt has a third son who'll be only too pleased to blow holes in you.'

'I'll take that chance,' Buck said.

'Then I'll go with you,' Moose said.

'You're needed here,' Buck told him, but avoided suggesting that the attack might be repeated. 'Anyway, remember, Walt reckons you killed his two boys.'

'I'll come with you,' Casey said. 'I'm

still the law.'

'Bad idea.' Buck was adamant. 'Best I go alone.'

Sam looked as if she was going to say something, but clamped her lips shut. Buck tried to read her expression. Did she fear for his safety, or had she already made up her mind to quit? He preferred the first option.

'If you're dead set on getting killed,' Casey said.

Sam found her voice. 'If you're determined, Buck, it's late. Please stay here for the night. You can use the spare bed in the bunkhouse. I'll cook you a good breakfast in the morning.'

The offer was tempting and Buck saw the wisdom of her suggestion. 'Sunup it is, then.'

Sam turned her attention to the marshal. 'I hope you'll stay and join us, Casey. It's too late for you to think of returning to town. I'm sure Moose can fix up another bed. You'll be comfortable there.'

Moose nodded. 'I'll be pleased to have

the company.'

The marshal needed no further encouragement. 'OK, Sam. I'll take the body back at first light.'

'What're ya doing with Clint?' Buck asked.

'Funny thing is, I dunno what to do with him,' Casey admitted. 'He wasn't involved in the bank hold-up an' there ain't no poster out on him. I've charged him with assault so's I kin hold him for a while.' He rubbed his head where Clint had hit him.

'Also he was with the outlaw gang an' was unlucky enough to have his horse stumble, but I can't tie him in with anything that I can arrest him for.'

'Didn't trouble you overmuch when you arrested me.' Buck grinned.

'Yeah, I sorta regret doing that,' Casey admitted. 'Wouldn't have been given a sore head.'

'If you can't hold him you'll have to let him go.'

'It don't sit right with me, but that's what I'll need to do, I reckon.'

Buck nodded. 'Do me a favour, Casey. Hold him till I get a chance to talk to him again.'

'Yep. Suits me. If you don't get yerself killed first,' he added.

'D'you figure that's what the rancher will have in mind for me?'

Casey hesitated. 'Dunno. He's not a killer 's far as I know, but he is ambitious and, some say, ruthless.' He glanced at Sam. 'He could've driven Sam out if he'd bin of a mind to do so, but he had other ideas.'

Sam blushed. 'I have never given him any encouragement,' she said. 'Sometimes I don't understand men.'

Buck said quickly, 'No good guessing. We'll know more tomorrow when I get back.' He exchanged glances with Casey, who was about to say something but changed his mind.

15

At sunup Casey set off back to town with the dead man. Moose cleared away the debris from the burned-out barn while Buck, in spite of further objections from Sam, set his horse towards the ranch of Walt Grayson. After a moment's hesitation he had buckled on his gun.

He was no nearer than half a mile from the ranch when he realized he had an escort. Two burly men on horseback closed in on him, one on each side, and silently kept pace with him. He tried several times to strike up a conversation but the men, sitting ramrod upright in their saddles, kept looking straight ahead.

They rode in this way until the ranch house came into view. Buck reined in to take in the splendid sight. The building sat on a slight rise, a lush valley falling away from the large wooden veranda. From there Walt Grayson could gaze upon the beginning of his vast ranch, an open, uninterrupted vista.

One of the guides tapped Buck's horse to set it forward again and went ahead while the second man trailed behind. They were taking no chances, it seemed.

At the front of the house, where a covered porch guarded the entrance from the worst of the weather, Buck was ordered to dismount.

'Gun!' The larger of his escorts held out his hand. The meaning was clear. Buck was not to be armed when he met the great man. Buck saw no future in ignoring the command. He removed his gunbelt and handed it across, dismounted and climbed the steps leading up to the massive front door.

At that moment the door opened and Walt Grayson stood there, a smile of welcome on his face.

'Been expecting you,' he said. He held out his hand and shook Buck's as if they had been lifelong friends.

Buck, who had been expecting aggression, was confused by the amiability of the man.

'Of, course, you would know I was on my way,' Buck said.

'Soon as you left the main trail.'

'And you didn't try to stop me?'

Walt guffawéd. 'Why should I? You're no danger to me.' He dismissed the two men with a wave of his hand and led the way inside and into a large room. It was a luxurious home, from the soft, expensive carpet on the floors to the mahogany furniture and leather armchairs.

Buck sank into one of the cushioned chairs and watched as a young woman of about twenty years of age brought in a tray holding a decanter and some glasses that clinked against each other as her hands shook slightly.

'Careful, you clumsy girl!' the rancher bellowed. 'Leave it there. I'll see to it.'

The girl frowned, set the tray on a table by the wall and left.

'My first wife's daughter,' Walt explained with a dismissive wave of his hand. 'Works in the kitchen.' He filled two glasses with the pale amber liquid. 'Whisky, specially imported from Scotland,' he said. 'Not to everyone's taste, but let me know what you think. Let it just trickle across your tongue and down your throat.'

Buck drank slowly. He was used to the coarse flavour of cheap saloon whiskey and was surprised by the silky smoothness of the drink. 'I could get used to it, I reckon,' he said, but refused a refill.

Walt sipped his own drink. 'Cigar?' He offered Buck a slim cheroot. Buck accepted but held it without lighting it.

He was aware that the rancher had been studying him, quite openly and without betraying his thoughts. He let the silence lengthen as he in turn tried to assess the rancher who just now was appearing to be pleasant and hospitable. As he looked closer he thought he saw meanness in the eyes that didn't sit well with the smile and the gentle tone of voice. Walt was the first to speak.

'Perhaps you'd care to tell me why you've come to visit me. You did, after all, shoot one of my sons, and now he and his brother are dead. In the circumstances I'm certain you wouldn't expect me to be pleased to see you.'

Buck gave him a hard stare. 'I ain't complaining about your hospitality. Yeah, I put a slug into your son's leg when he was trying to kill me,' he said evenly, going on to explain how it had happened. 'I don't cotton to men harassing young ladies, which is what both your sons were doing. I did what I had to do and I'd do it again in the same situation.'

'Except that now they're dead.'

'Yeah, they're dead, and I regret that. But they took it into their heads to give me a beating an' were gonna kill me.' He gave an account of how he had been tied up and assaulted. 'If I hadn't been rescued I'd not be here now.'

'And my sons would still be alive.'

'Like I said, I'm sorry.'

'I'm sure you are. But if that's what you've come all this way to tell me you've wasted your time.'

'It's not all.' Buck, who had been toying with the cigar he'd been given earlier, now took time to light it. When he was satisfied he said, 'Last night two of your men attacked the homestead of Sam Merryman. It was lucky that I was near by and we were able to kill one who called himself Greg. We chased the other away.'

The rancher held up his hands in horror. 'What in tarnation makes you think I would send them? Sam and I have had our differences for sure, but I'd most certainly not send men to attack her.'

'I reckoned they were from this ranch.'

'I doubt that very much.'

'The one who got away will be nursing a slug.'

'Then it should be easy to prove one way or the other.'

'And if he works for you?'

'I shall see to it that he's suitably punished. And then dismissed.'

'You're telling me that you had nothing to do with the attack?'

'That's what I'm telling you if you'd pay attention to what I'm saying.' Walt gave a tug on the bell pull again. When his step-daughter came back into the room, he said, 'Tell Wilf I want to see him now.'

His emphasis on the last word was not lost on the girl.

Wilf came at once, removing his Stetson as he entered the room. He was young with a boyish face, seeming at ease in front of the big man. Walt turned to Buck.

'This is my third son. Maybe you'll get to know him better later on.' Then to his son he said, 'Wilf, d'you know anything about one of our men being killed yesterday? Apparently his name was Greg.'

Wilf shook his head. 'No, Pa. There ain't none of our men missing.'

'Is one of them wounded?'

'No, Pa. I'd know about it fer sure.'

'And you would've told me, wouldn't you, of any attack on any homestead?'

'Sure, Pa. What homestead?'

'Sam Merryman's.'

'No, Pa. You told us —'

'I know what I told you.'

Wilf looked as if he was about to leave, but his pa signalled to him to remain.

Walt studied Buck's face. 'You must've been misinformed.'

Buck stared at both men. 'Yeah, must've.'

'You don't sound convinced.'

'I know what you're telling me, that's all. Mebbe the marshal will have a better idea when he gets the body back to town.'

'Did you kill him?'

'Yeah, an' I put a slug in the other one.' Buck thought it best to keep things simple.

'You've been busy, then.'

Buck showed his exasperation. 'He talked before he died. Not only that but he left his horse behind.'

'My brand?'

'Nope.'

'Whose, then?'

'Didn't recognize it.'

'I see.' The rancher folded his arms. 'So you immediately jumped to the wrong conclusion. Seems to me that whoever those men were they got what they deserved.'

Buck sensed a definite edge to the rancher's tone as he continued, 'And now, if you'll excuse me, I have many hours of work to get through.' He stood up. 'I think we understand each other. This meeting is over.'

Buck also rose to his feet. 'I'll take my leave, then.'

'On the contrary,' Walt purred. 'I think you'll be with us for quite a while yet. Is that right, Wilf?'

Buck turned his gaze to the young man and immediately let out a gasp. Wilf, with a smile that stretched his lips, was holding a gun, and it was pointing unerringly at Buck's chest.

'What …?'

'This way,' Wilf said with a snarl.

'Is this how you treat your guests?'

'It grieves me to do this,' the rancher said, 'but you see, you seem to have been partly responsible for killing his two brothers. I'm sure you'll understand that he's very upset.'

'I didn't kill your brothers,' Buck grated, swinging back to Wilf. 'I've already explained to your pa. They were gonna kill me.'

Walt had almost lost interest in his

guest. 'I know who pulled the trigger and he'll pay for that. But you were there. That's enough.' He strode from the room.

Wilf beckoned Buck impatiently. 'Let's go.'

Buck shrugged, accepting that for the moment he had no choice. He also knew that his future was likely to be extremely short and unpleasant unless he could find a way out of this situation. The possibilities of that had to be very limited indeed.

Wilf directed him out of the house and towards a low barn.

'Before we get down to business,' Wilf said, his eyes lighting up with anticipation, 'I want you to meet someone.'

Buck looked around as he walked. The yard at the front of the house was neat and clean, the entrance being formed into a huge dome from several enormous timbers. There were few men here, but he could hear activity not far away. What men there were gazed at him with some amusement, acknowledging Wilf as he brandished his gun.

As they approached the barn Buck had

sight of the corral containing about half a dozen horses. He had time to note that his own mount had been placed there, the saddle and bridle having been removed.

He had no time to see more because a man had stepped out of the barn and now stood there with his hands on his hips.

'Grant!' Buck breathed, and rounded on Wilf. 'Yeah, I heard that your pa employs outlaws now.'

'Reckoned ya'd be pleased to see him.' Wilf laughed. 'Grant's bin with us fer a year or so now. What he does in his spare time ain't no concern of ours.'

Grant waited until Buck was a few feet away, then stepped forward and swung his fist. Buck tried to duck, but caught the blow on the side of his head. He went down, scrabbled to his feet again and drew back his own fist.

He didn't get the chance to retaliate as Wilf's gun took him on the other side of his head in a vicious blow. He went down again, and this time didn't get up.

In a daze he heard Wilf say, 'Easy, Grant. You kin have him when I've finished. Seems he couldn't wait to see ya agin. You'll both have a lot to talk over.'

'Leave some of him fer me, then,' Grant said. 'I've bin looking forward to this. My head still hurts.'

'If ya hear screams don't let it concern ya none.' Both men laughed at this great joke.

Wilf kicked Buck in the ribs. 'Git up! Git up or I'll drag ya by yer feet.'

Although Buck had been initially disabled by the blow on the head, he was recovering fast. He groaned realistically and stayed where he was, even when he felt Wilf grab at his ankles, pull him along the ground and into the barn.

He knew he had only one chance. If he messed it up he would be as good as dead. He watched through half-closed eyes as Wilf unhooked some rope from a hook in the wall and approached him with a gleam in his eyes. He allowed one hand to be pulled behind his back and felt the rope being placed around his wrist.

16

As Wilf grasped the other hand Buck acted. He whirled round and threw up his arm so that the rope now looped over Wilf's neck. He gave two rapid twists and pulled hard, tightening the loops. With his free hand he made a grab for Wilf's gun.

Wilf was quick to react. He let out a yell of fury and tried to ease the pressure on his windpipe. Buck twisted harder and tried to bring the Colt into play. Wilf's violent movements had loosened his hold on the butt and the Colt skidded across the floor, out of reach.

Praying that Wilf's shout would be interpreted as his own cry of pain Buck fought hard to subdue his opponent as quickly as possible in case someone came to investigate. Soon he had Wilf face down on the floor gasping for air. His knee was pressing down on the small of his back and he had one arm in a painful lock.

'Give up,' he hissed. 'Keep quiet an' I'll let you breathe. Make a sound an' I'll kill you.' It was an empty threat and he knew it.

Wilf managed a nod of his head.

Buck eased the rope, but still kept his knee in place and retained the arm lock to prevent Wilf from breaking free.

'Listen, you sonofabitch,' Buck grated. 'I'm gonna get off you, but you're gonna stay exactly where you are, an' you're gonna remain as quiet as a mouse. If you don't I'm gonna have to slip this knife into your back.' He pressed his finger between Wilf's shoulder blades, hoping it would feel like the blade he didn't possess.

He rose swiftly and, retaining his hold on the rope's end, he hurled himself across the floor and gathered up the gun, returning to stand above the prostrate man.

'Get on your feet!'

Wilf stood slowly, took a deep breath and screamed, 'Help!'

Buck laid the barrel across Wilf's skull. Wilf collapsed without a sound. Buck held his breath. Would the cry bring men running? He now had a gun but that would be of little use against those who might even now be rushing to Wilf's aid.

He peered through a crack in the cladding, saw men looking over towards the barn and laughing. He offered up a prayer of thanks. He had got away with it so far. Now what?

Without a horse he wasn't going to get very far. His own mount was a mere fifty yards away. In that distance, even if he raced at top speed, there would be time for many slugs to be sent in his direction.

He considered his options. It didn't take him long. He certainly had to do something. He couldn't stay where he was and he couldn't enter into a gun fight and survive for more than a minute.

He could change clothes with Wilf, since they were about the same size, then walk casually to the corral, saddle and mount his horse and ride out. As he said it to himself it sounded most unlikely that he would get away with that.

The second option was to make it un-observed over to the rear of the house. As he studied the layout of the ground he thought that might be possible. Then what?

But what happened when he reached the ranch house didn't seem as important as what action to take right now. Although he was mostly concerned about his own safety he hoped that he hadn't hit Wilf too hard. He bent over the still figure.

Wilf was breathing, but only just. His Stetson had fallen off and his hair was matted with blood. He didn't give the impression that he was going to recover soon, maybe not at all. Buck made him as comfortable as possible after removing his shirt and putting it on over his own. He picked up Wilf's hat and jammed it on his own head.

'Sorry, Wilf,' he murmured, went over to the half-open door and studied the ground between the barn and the house. It was planted partly as a well-kept vege-table garden, sheltered by a line of pines from the prevailing winds that would whip through in the season.

The trees were about twenty yards away from where he stood and he reckoned that if he could make it to them without being seen he could cover the remaining twenty yards more easily. A door there probably gave entry to the kitchen area where he could conceal himself while he thought out the next stage of his plan.

'Not much of a plan,' he muttered. 'Anyway, no good thinking about it.' With a final glance at Wilf and a quick survey of who might be watching, he launched himself out of the barn and walked swiftly, hoping not to draw attention to himself.

The trees seemed a long way off, but he reached them without hearing a cry of discovery. He was breathing hard and, as he rested against a trunk, his head throbbed and his ribs ached where he had been kicked.

From the trees he made it to the door, praying that it wasn't locked. He put his ear to the wood, listening briefly before turning the handle and slipping through. He closed the door and leaned his back against it.

He was in a large preparation and cooking area. He was alone. Or thought he was.

Too late he watched as a figure rose from a seat near the window. As the face came into the light he recognized the young woman who had only a short time ago brought in the drinks to the rancher's study.

He tried to smile as if everything was normal, but the girl opened her mouth as if to scream. He held up his hand and was relieved when the girl closed her mouth without uttering a word. She put her finger to her lips for silence and indicated that there was another person in the next room.

For the space of half a minute Buck and the girl eyed each other, then she smiled coyly and beckoned, pointing to a third door that Buck had not noticed. He walked across the room as the girl opened the door and urged him through.

He found himself in a small parlour with shelves around the wall, all stacked high with utensils. He whirled. Was this a trick to lock him in? But the girl followed him.

'My name's Molly,' she whispered. 'I know who you are. I heard them talking about you. They were going to kill you.'

This was not news to Buck, although he might have hoped that his treatment would end with just a beating.

'Thanks, Molly,' he said softly.

'You've got to get away from here.'

Buck nodded. That wasn't news, either. 'How?'

'You need a horse.'

Buck nodded again.

'I'm going to help you, but you'll have to wait here while I go and talk to Joe.'

'Who's Joe?'

From the way Molly blushed the answer was obvious.

'OK,' he said.

Could he trust her? And what about Joe? There was no reason that Buck could see for either of them to risk their own position on his account. He sat on a flimsy wooden stool, held Wilf's gun on his lap and checked it over. It was in fine condition with five chambers full, the sixth one empty. He'd use it if he had to, but he'd have to make every slug count.

After five minutes Molly returned. Her face was strained.

'Your horse is at the rail by the front door,' she said with an edge of desperation. 'If you go now you should be able to get to it without being seen. Pull your Stetson low and you may be able to ride out without being challenged. Joe's keeping the passageway clear as best he can.'

Buck rose and placed a hand on her arm.

'Thanks, Molly.' He wanted to ask why she was doing this, but Molly was urging him to hurry. He jammed the Colt in his waist band, tugged at his hat and followed Molly's directions, smiling his thanks. The passageway was covered with thick-pile carpeting, so his footsteps were soundless. He reached the door without being challenged, opened it and peered out. A

192

few men were working some fifty paces away, but their attention was focused on the task they were doing.

He walked down the steps, approached his horse and tested the cinch in case someone had thought to spring a surprise on him. Everything seemed normal as he mounted and rode calmly towards the yard entrance, beyond which was freedom.

It was at that moment that a shout went up from the direction of the barn. It was a yell of anger from Wilf, who had recovered and had staggered to the barn door to raise the alarm. Buck kept moving easily so as not to draw attention to himself, and had reached the entrance before the shouts had turned in his direction.

He risked a glance behind and saw men pointing and running for their horses.

'I'll give 'em a run for their money,' he muttered and, lying low in the saddle, he urged his mount to a full gallop.

Guns cracked and bullets came his way, none of them close enough to worry him. But he knew that wouldn't last because he had only a short head start on his pursuers. The chestnut was a stayer rather than being made for speed. It would not be long before someone would be near enough to aim more accurately with their shots.

He glanced behind again as he set his horse down the trail. Two men only were following hard on his heels. Ahead, about half a mile away, a high escarpment offered a possible place where he could make a stand. He regretted his decision not to take Wilf's gunbelt. Five bullets for two men. Maybe that would be enough if they didn't get him first.

He was now only about one hundred yards from the safety of the rocks, but the shooting was becoming more dangerous as the men closed in on him. A final burst of speed and he would have reached temporary safety, but his heart lurched as he saw another rider come into view around the corner ahead of him.

There was nowhere to go but straight on. He could use one of his precious slugs on this new threat, which would leave two each for the men behind. He raised the Colt, but lowered it quickly as he recognized the rider.

'Casey,' he breathed, as he reached the first of the rocks. Then, 'Get under cover!' he roared, realizing that the marshal had not fully recognized the danger. He flung himself from the saddle and crouched down behind a rock fall, using his precious supply of bullets to deter his pursuers and give time for Casey to reach concealment.

Buck indicated his gun, telling the marshal that he was out of shells. Casey, who had also dismounted, had slipped his Winchester from its scabbard and tossed it across.

'You any good with that?'

Buck caught the rifle easily, turned it towards the approaching men and fired off two rounds.

'Stop where you are!' he shouted.

There was a fusillade of shots in reply. The men had taken cover.

Then came a voice, full of the authority of the law:

'This is Marshal Casey Humble. Turn

and go back. This man is my prisoner an' I'm takin' him in. You have no business here.'

This was a long speech that seemed to have little immediate effect until one of the men yelled back:

'We were gonna bring him in, Marshal. He's a dangerous man. Best if we go with ya so there won't be no trouble.'

Casey gave a hollow laugh. 'I've dealt with dangerous men afore now an' I'm still alive to tell the tale. I reckon to stay that way. You're interfering with the law an' that's an offence. Go home.'

'Yer out of yer bailiwick.'

Casey yelled back. 'If you're so sure of that come an' tell me to my face.'

'This ain't nothin' to do with you.'

'You neither. Tell your boss if he wants to talk to me he knows where to find me.'

Buck heard the two men arguing with each other. There seemed to be a difference of opinion, but eventually the same man said:

'Right, Marshal. We're leavin'. But you kin expect that visit from our boss, who won't be well pleased.'

The men remounted and rode away, leaving Buck feeling mightily relieved that a full confrontation had been avoided. But for how long? He allowed the men to disappear into the distance before he rose and walked over to the marshal. He held out his hands in mock surrender.

'I guess ya wanna put the cuffs on, me being a dangerous man.'

Casey remained serious. 'What went on back there?'

Buck chewed his lip. 'Casey, I'm getting tired of being attacked, threatened, beaten, shot at an' chased, which is what I've been since I set foot in Rymansville. This ain't a friendly town.' He jerked his thumb in the direction of the ranch. 'I reckon they were gonna kill me, an' if you hadn't come along they might've succeeded.'

He stepped into the saddle as Casey did the same, and they set off side by side at an easy gait towards Sam's homestead, each glancing frequently over his shoulder to make sure they weren't being followed.

Casey smiled. 'Yeah, I can see how you might think like that,' he said. 'I've been marshal here fer nigh on twenty years. I was appointed on account of the council figured I'd play the game the way they and Walt Grayson wanted it. That is, keep the town quiet during the day and let it go wild at sundown.'

'An' did you?'

'I did. That arrangement suited everyone, including me. The stores and the saloon made plenty o' dollars an' the ranchers' men knew they could let their hair down. Even old Manny, the undertaker, saw his business growing. Any damage was paid for by Walt Grayson.'

Buck nodded. 'Sounds like you don't cotton to the idea any more.'

Casey was silent for a full minute. 'Tell the truth, Buck, it took a lady of my acquaintance to make me see what I shoulda bin doing all along. That is, I shoulda acted like an officer of the law.' He fingered the silver star on his shirt. 'That's what I intend to do from here on in.'

'You're up against strong opposition,

seems to me,' Buck observed.

'Yep.'

'But this lady? Have you good intentions?'

Casey guffawed. 'That's one way o' putting it. But, no, since she's already married I have to be patient. Her husband's likely to drink hisself to death or get lead poisoning afore long.'

They were now close to the homestead and were relieved to see that everything looked normal. Even the remains of the barn had been cleared away.

The wagon with the tarp covering the dead man was still in the yard.

'Thought you'd taken that into town,' Buck said.

Casey grinned. 'I turned back when I realized what a doggone fool you were to go to the ranch without someone to watch your back.'

'I owe you,' Buck said. 'What're you gonna do now?'

'What I shoulda done earlier. Time that body's put in the ground.'

'I'll stay here a while,' Buck told him.

'Walt Grayson might take it into his head to pay Sam another visit. We'll be ready for him.'

17

After a brief stop for coffee and some of Sam's biscuits Casey set off for Rymansville. He was wary, although he didn't expect trouble. His message to Walt Grayson, if the men had delivered it as he thought they would, was likely to bring the rancher into town for a confrontation. Whether he would come alone or be accompanied by some of his gunmen would not matter. The marshal would be ready.

He enjoyed the journey on the wagon, something he rarely had the opportunity to do, and he gave rein to his thoughts, delving deeper into his way of life than he had ever done.

The woman he had spoken of to Buck was very often in his thoughts and he drew pictures in his mind of their future together, knowing that this was unlikely. They had met secretly and passionately a few times, but that was a dangerous luxury that could not be continued now that her husband had begun to suspect.

Casey reached the undertaker without coming to any conclusion.

'Best act quickly on this one, Manny,' he said. 'An' don't concern yourself with the hole in his chest. He was killed legal in self-defence.'

'With a rifle?' Manny queried, as he looked closer.

'I'm tellin' you. Self-defence. I should know on account of I was there,' Casey lied.

Manny took a quick breath. 'Bullet holes don't worry me none,' he said quickly. 'I've seen more'n most folk. They git buried with the rest of the remains.'

Casey grunted and rode down the main drag to his office. He knew at once that there was someone inside and he drew his Colt as he looped the reins. Then he mounted the steps and pushed open the door. Sarah Finney was perched nervously on the edge of the chair with her hands clasped tightly together. There was an air of desperation about her that was not lost on the marshal.

'Sarah! What're you doing here?'

'Sorry, Casey,' she said. 'I had to come. I didn't know where else to go.'

He studied her face and saw fresh bruises. Anger and desire welled within him. 'What happened?'

'Baff was more drunk than usual. He thought I should have been quicker with the chores. An' we've been arguing about selling up to Walt Grayson.'

'How'd you get away?'

'I took the wagon into town for fresh supplies.'

'Where is he now?'

He could have answered his own question as he heard heavy footsteps outside and peered out of the window.

'That's Baff now. Quick! Hide in there.' He hurried her through the door leading to the cells.

Casey returned to stand and gaze without speaking as the big man barged into his office and planted his feet in front of the lawman's dusk.

'Ya've gotta find my wife for me.'

Casey raised his eyebrows questioningly. 'I ain't gotta do anything.'

'You're the law, ain't ya? Are ya just gonna stand there?' Baff Finney thumped the desk with an oversized fist, making the contents rattle. 'My taxes pay yer wages, Marshal. My wife goes missin' an' I expect help from the law. She could've bin murdered.'

'And who might've done such a thing?' the marshal asked. His low opinion of the man was evident in his tone of voice.

'I've got enemies. They wanna hurt me. I can't manage the farm without Sarah.'

'How long's she been gone?'

'Since this morning. Said she was coming into town fer supplies. Shoulda been back long ago.'

'Where's the wagon now?'

'Outside the saloon where I found it. She wasn't with it.'

'How long ago was that?'

'No time at all.'

From the smell on Baff's breath Casey reckoned that it was several whiskeys ago.

The marshal lit and took a long drag on a cigar as if he was contemplating what action to take to find the missing woman. That was the last thing on his mind just then.

'I'll look into it,' he said at last and blew smoke into the room.

Baff Finney leaned forward and rested both hands on the desk, bringing his face close. 'Not good enough.'

Strong whiskey fumes caused Casey to draw back. Baff Finney didn't scare him.

'I've got some questions of my own,' he growled. 'When I last saw Sarah she was wearing several new bruises on her face. D'you know anything about that?'

Finney shook his head. 'Must've bin kicked by one o' them hosses, stupid bitch.'

Casey stared hard into the bloodshot eyes of the man. 'Not the first time folk have noticed such things. You must have some wild stock up there.'

'It happens.'

'I've heard folk say the marks look more like they'd been done by knuckles.

They say you treat her bad. Is that so?'

Finney glared. 'Let 'em say it to my face. Is that what you believe?' His fleshy face took on an angry red. His eyes screwed to mere slits.

Casey squared up to him. 'Yep. It's what I believe. You're a bully. You like to beat up women. I reckon you might've killed Sarah yourself. Did you?'

Finney opened his mouth to reply but he stopped, his eyes widening as the door from the cells swung open and Sarah walked through.

'I've heard enough. I can't have you lying for me, Casey,' she said. She swung round to face her husband. 'I'm leaving you, Baff. I'm selling up and leaving you.'

'Ya can't leave me, you stupid bitch. Ya coming back with me right now.' He took a step towards her. Casey barred his path.

'Sarah's safe now an' she's gonna stay that way.' He was prepared for the man to swing at him but was taken by surprise when Finney, with unexpected speed, drew his .45.

'Git outta my way!'

Casey had his back to Sarah and did not see her produce a single-barrelled derringer from her coat. Before he could stop her she had thrust the weapon into her husband's chest and pulled the trigger.

Her husband gasped once, tilted slowly, and was dead before he hit the floor like a felled tree.

Sarah and Casey stared at each other for several long minutes. Sarah was first to break the silence.

'I've been wanting to do that for years. Never had the courage. You'd better arrest me.'

The marshal grinned. 'Arrest you?' He stared down at the dead man whose gun was still in his hand. 'Nope. You just saved my life. Clearest case of self-defence I ever seen.'

'What are you going to do, then?'

The marshal's grin broadened. 'I'm gonna marry you, if you'll still have me.'

Sarah came into his open arms. 'Try and stop me!'

Only now was Casey aware of the yelling that was coming from the cells.

'Hey! Marshal! What's goin' on out there?' Clint's voice was loud and strident.

'I forgot about him,' Casey said. He opened the intervening door and shouted, 'Shuddup, Clint.' He turned back to Sarah.

'It'll be best if you go now while I have a serious talk with my prisoner. We'll keep our relationship quiet till I've sorted all this out. Call in on the undertaker and tell him that I've got a dead body here.'

Sarah kissed him on the cheek, gave a quick glance at the body of her husband.

'He was a bad man, Casey. And a stupid one. He thought he could sell out to Walt Grayson for a good price. He got some men to put a scare into Sam Merryman so she would sell. Said it was all for the best. He couldn't see it. Walt would have taken it all from him. I suppose I'll have to give up the farm now and Walt will get it cheap.'

Casey held her hand. 'Not yet, Sarah. Don't sell yet. Wait awhile. The rancher might not get everything his own way.'

Sarah waited for him to go on. When he didn't explain she kissed him and gave him a last look of trust and hope. Without another glance at the body of her husband she left.

Casey went to see Clint.

'What was the shootin' about?' Clint asked.

'Not your concern.' The marshal produced a set of keys and opened the cell door.

'Ya lettin' me go, Marshal?'

'Haven't made up my mind yet.'

'What charge are ya holding me on?'

'None of your business.'

He led the way into the office. Clint stopped dead when he saw the body. 'Who's the lucky man?'

Casey patted his gun. 'He was trying to escape, so don't get any ideas about that yerself. I'd shoot you before you reached the door.'

Clint shrugged. 'What makes you think I'd try to escape? Yer deputy serves up a good meal. Best one I've had fer a long time.'

Casey held up his hand for silence. 'I haven't much time, Clint. There's likely to be some action here before long and I've got some questions for you.'

'I might not have the answers.'

'It'll be better for you if you have.'

'How about a slug o' that whiskey, then?'

Casey filled two glasses and pushed one across the desk. 'The names of the members of your gang,' he said bluntly. 'An' don't bother to lie to me.'

'I don't tell lies, Marshal.'

'The names of your gang!'

'I don't have a gang,' Clint said. 'Don't ya recall what I told ya?'

'We caught you at the hideout,' Casey reminded him. 'All the other varmints escaped. I know you weren't at the raid on the bank. I'd like to know who was.'

'What's in it fer me?'

'I'll tell the judge at your trial how co-operative you were. You're likely to face a long prison sentence otherwise.'

Casey was desperate to hurry this along, but he knew instinctively that if he was too eager Clint could clam up. He let the silence lengthen while Clint downed the whiskey and put a flame to the cigar that Casey had offered.

'OK,' Clint said. 'I'll tell ya, but ya'll have to give me protection.'

'I can do that if necessary.' Casey wrote with a stub of a pencil as Clint gave him several names, although Clint didn't tell him much that he didn't already know.

'You'll keep yer promise?' Clint asked.

'Better'n that,' Casey told him. 'I'm letting you go.'

Clint's expression was hard to read. 'Why in hell would ya wanna do that?'

'I was asked by a friend of yours.'

'I ain't got no friends.'

'Name of Buck. Reckon you might've known him as Ray. You gave me a sore head when you took him from my jail.'

'Yeah, I recall. Sorry 'bout yer head.'

'I'm sure you are.'

'So I'm free to go?'

'Yep. But only till I want you again.'

'What the hell does that mean?' Clint asked, his eyes wide open.

Casey had always intended to release his prisoner, mainly on account of having no firm evidence against him. And now he didn't want a prisoner in the cells when Walt Grayson came calling.

'It means I'll wanna see you again when the judge comes next week.'

Clint frowned. 'What the hell! What if I ain't around at the time?'

'In that event,' Casey said slowly, 'I reckon the judge'll have to move on without sentencing you.'

'Thanks, Marshal,' Clint said in a tone that indicated that he hadn't thanked anyone for a long time. 'Ya sure ain't what they say ya are.'

Casey managed a grin. 'An' what do they say I am, Clint?'

'D'ya want the truth, Marshal?'

'You told me you don't tell lies. What do folk say 'bout me?'

'That ya take orders from the council an' that they take orders from Walt Grayson.'

Casey pushed him out through the door. 'They were probably right,

Clint. But that's about to change. Now vamoose.'

He stood and watched while Clint scuttled down the street. 'It probably has already changed,' he muttered. 'P'raps they don't know it yet.'

18

The sun was hot, but Moose hardly seemed to notice it. Neither did he appear to be too concerned with being out in the open in the event that the rancher's men returned. Buck was more vigilant and, as he forked hay, he caught sight of the riders as they breasted the hill. There were three of them.

'Moose,' he called. 'Time to get under cover.'

There was no knowing at that distance who the men were, but he could hazard a good guess. 'Walt Grayson's paying us another visit, I reckon,' he said.

He led the way indoors, picked up the Winchester and laid it on the window ledge. 'I'll see what he wants this time,' he told Sam.

'Best if I meet him,' she said, for by now it was easy to recognize Walt Grayson's bay. 'Please keep out of sight. You won't be too popular with him just now. You're supposed to have been taken into town by the marshal as a prisoner, remember.'

Buck reluctantly agreed, although it was not in his nature to hide from trouble, and he was ready to show his face, and his gun if necessary.

The three men reined in twenty feet from the door. The rancher dismounted and approached on foot as Sam stepped outside to meet him.

The rancher's first words were lost to Buck as he recognized one of the riders. 'Grant,' he growled under his breath. 'Seems I can't get rid of you.'

'Two visits in as many days,' Sam was saying. 'To what do I owe the pleasure?'

'As charming and hospitable as ever,' Walt said smoothly. 'Are you inviting me in?'

'I don't recall doing so,' Sam said, although the directness of her reply was tempered by a smile. 'I'd rather we conducted our business out here.' She indicated two old rocking-chairs on the small veranda. 'We could sit in the shade.'

Walt accepted that invitation and they both settled themselves.

'Can I offer you and your men some refreshments?' Sam asked.

Walt shook his head. 'Thank you, no. If you'll cooperate with me we will be moving on. I'll come to the point. A man came to my ranch, threatened me and injured my son. He is the same man who was involved in the murder of my other two sons. If you are giving him shelter here I have to ask you to hand him over to me.'

Sam stared at him. 'If that man happened to be here and you took him away, what would you do to him?'

'Why,' the rancher beamed, 'I'd take him straight into town and hand him over to the marshal. It's the law, you see, and I'm a law-abiding citizen.'

'That's good to know, Walt. But it seems your journey has been wasted. Maybe you should go and talk with Casey Humble, though I'm sure he has everything under control.'

'I'm sure he has,' the rancher said. 'But

likely not as I want it.'

He stared directly at Sam for a long minute and shifted his gaze towards his two men as if considering his next action. Buck checked the Colt he had taken from Wilf and picked up the rifle. Moose had grasped an axe handle. If the rancher and his men forced their way into the house they would meet strong resistance.

'Sam,' Walt said at last, 'I've never done anything to hurt you but my patience is running low. I lost two sons to a trigger-happy coyote and I intend to see justice done. He's going to swing for it. If the law won't do it I will.' He stood up. Sam rose and faced him.

'Walt, I've never had any quarrel with you, but burning down my barn! What was that supposed to mean?'

'That wasn't with my knowledge. My third son may have taken it into his head to do something like that, thinking it was what I wanted. All three of my boys sometimes acted without thinking. Now two of them are dead and the third has had his head cracked with the butt of a gun.' He stood.

'You can hardly lay the blame for that at my door, Walt.' She waited for him to say something more. When he didn't she said, 'Thank you for calling in, but you hardly needed to bring your gunmen with you. Seems like you've wasted your time. I'm sorry I can't help you.'

The rancher appeared to make a decision.

'Before I leave will you allow me to look over your cabin? I need to make sure you're not harbouring a killer.'

Sam shook her head vigorously. 'No, Walt, you may not. Nobody comes into my home without I ask them in. No killer is hiding here. You will have to take my word for that.'

Walt took a step back as if he had been physically slapped.

'I'll have to insist, Sam. It will only take a minute. You must understand my reasons for wanting to do so.' He signalled to his men who dismounted and stood ready.

The movement as they loosened the

guns in their holsters was not lost on Sam. She held her ground.

'I said no! You're not setting foot inside my home, Walt. Nor are those two men. I must ask you to leave.'

The rancher showed no inclination to go. 'Sam, I insist. I have to do what has to be done.'

Within the house Buck had heard enough. He knew he was walking into danger by showing himself, but he was weary of skulking in the shadows, hiding behind a woman's skirts. He flung the door wide and strode out to stand beside Sam.

Moose was only a step behind. Both he and Buck held guns in their hands. He handed the Winchester to Sam, who took it and levered a round into the chamber.

'That's far enough, Walt,' Buck growled. To the two men he said, 'Keep your hands off your guns if you value your lives.'

Hatred flared in Grant's eyes.

Either the men didn't value their lives or they thought they could draw and fire before Buck could pull on the trigger.

They were mistaken. Their hands snaked down with such speed that Buck was almost taken by surprise. He fired just as their guns cleared leather and Grant staggered back with blood spurting from his chest.

Moose had also fired a split second after Buck. His slug found its mark just as the second gunman pulled the trigger. The slug aimed at Moose went wide and hit Sam in the leg. She spun, dropped the rifle and leaned weakly against the wall.

'No!' Buck cried and rushed to support her.

'You!' Walt yelled. He drew his Colt, raised it and pointed it at Buck. 'Take your hands off Sam and step away.'

Buck was too busy trying to stem the bleeding to take any notice.

'Right!' Walt screamed. 'I'll drop you where you stand.'

His finger tightened, but before he could exert the final pressure Moose fired, his slug entering Walt's hip.

With a cry of pain the rancher dropped his weapon and held both hands to the wound. Moose stepped forward, picked up the gun and helped him to a chair. Buck looked round.

'What in tarnation happened there?'

'He was gonna put some lead in you,' Moose said. 'So I put some in him.'

'Second time ya've saved my life,' Buck said. His gaze wandered out into the yard where two bodies lay, one barely moving, the other seemingly dead. 'We'll see to them soon's we've got Sam and Walt comfortable.'

Between them Buck and Moose helped Sam into the house where they placed her in a chair. Buck examined the wound. Moose returned to carry the rancher in.

Buck said, 'Sorry, Sam, I'm gonna have to tear your dress a little.'

When she nodded he carefully pulled the fabric away, revealing a tear in the flesh that was running with blood. 'Bullet went right through,' he told her. 'Some damage but it missed the bone.'

Sam managed a smile. 'There're some clean sheets in the cupboard.'

Moose brought them over and Sam

allowed Buck to bind her leg.

'Thanks, Buck. I'll be all right now.' He knew she was in pain, but no complaint passed her lips. 'You'd best go and check on Walt. I think he's worse than I am.'

He soon discovered she was right and that the rancher was not such an easy patient. The damage to his hip was severe although there was little bleeding. Moose had laid him on a makeshift bed.

'We'll need to get you both to town,' Buck told him. 'D'ya reckon you can travel that far?'

Walt moaned. His face was white and his breathing laboured as he tried to fight the pain.

'Get the doc here,' he grated. 'An' get him now. I'm not travelling anywhere.'

Buck glanced over at Sam. 'You all right if I do that?'

She nodded. 'Moose will stay with us. Best bring the undertaker as well.'

Buck checked on the two bodies in the yard, both of them now without a sign of life, and saddled up quickly. Although he didn't like leaving Sam and Moose alone he reckoned there would be no more unwelcome visitors to worry about. He set off at an easy lope.

19

The sun was low as Casey Humble peered out through the window of his office. Deputy Jesse France and another man stood back. They all three held their rifles at the ready.

'No sign of Walt Grayson or anybody else,' Casey said. 'Mebbe we've got it wrong.'

No sooner had he spoken than footsteps sounded on the boardwalk and someone attempted to open the door. It had been secured from the inside.

'Open up, Marshal,' Buck called and pounded on the wood panelling. 'It's me, Buck Norris. The notorious outlaw.'

Casey pulled back the bolts and pulled the door open. 'OK, Buck. You alone?'

'Yep,' Buck said.

'Come on in, but keep yer hands where I can see them.'

Buck stepped into the room and

gazed around. 'What's the armoury for? Expectin' a siege?'

The marshal smiled faintly. 'You could say that. What're you doin' here?'

'Come to get the undertaker and the doc. They should both be high-tailing it out to Sam's place right now.'

Concern showed on Casey's face. 'Sam hurt?'

'Yeah, but she's OK. The rancher got hit an' he's real bad.'

'Walt Grayson? What's bin going on?'

Buck gave a brief explanation. 'I don't reckon that Walt's intention was any more than to hunt me down. If he hadn't found me there he'd've come gunning for you.'

The marshal relaxed. 'Put yer guns down, boys. Looks like we ain't gonna get visitors after all.' He turned to Buck. 'Since you arrived in town there's bin nothing but shootin' and killin'.'

'Ain't no fault of mine,' Buck remonstrated.

This time the marshal's smile was more expansive. 'Never said it was. Fact is you've done us all a favour. 'Specially me.'

'I'm mighty pleased to hear that, Marshal,' Buck said. 'That mean ya ain't gonna lock me up after all?'

The marshal signalled to one of his deputies to get the coffee on the stove. His smile faded.

'This matter ain't finished yet. Injured or not, Walt Grayson is gonna be as mad as a wounded grizzly. He'll still be wanting revenge for his two sons an' he won't stop till he gets it.'

'He's gotta understand there was no choice. Those two wild jackasses were gonna kill me and Moose.'

'He won't see it that way. He comes from a hard school. He worked for a sheepherder when he was young. Beaten and starved and paid nothing.

'When Walt was old enough he killed the man, stole his sheep, sold them and went to work as a cowpuncher. He married the rancher's daughter. Some folk say he killed the rancher, although he claims the death was accidental. Then he took control of the ranch.'

'He's married?' Buck expressed his surprise.

The marshal gave a dry laugh. 'His wife also met with an accident.'

'And that's the same man who's made no secret of his intention to marry Sam?'

'Yep.'

'That's the one good thing outta all this. He met his match in Sam.'

'No knowin' what he'll do when he's pushed.'

'Well, he managed to get her shot. I'm goin' back.'

'At least stay for a cup of coffee.'

Buck shook his head. 'Nope. I'll have one at Sam's place.' He turned to leave.

'Wait!' The marshal's voice had in it a tone that caused Buck to hesitate.

'What is it?

'There's somethin' you should know before you go.'

'Yeah?'

'I've had word that your brother's headed this way.'

Buck gasped. 'He said he'd find me,

but it's been eleven years.'

'And he's been a bad boy in that time,' Casey said. 'Thought I should warn you, because I'll arrest him if he comes here.'

'Would you have to?'

'Yep. And I wouldn't have you stand in my way.'

'Thanks, Marshal. I'll keep a look out for him.'

'But,' Casey said, grinning widely, 'that's only if I'm still in office at the time. Can't speak fer Jesse here.'

'I'll bear that in mind. Now I must get back to Sam.'

Buck flung the door wide, nearly ripping off the remaining hinge, and strode out.

Casey grinned at Jesse. 'I'd better go and break the good news to the town council.'

The Rymansville council took the news about Walt Grayson with grey faces.

'Who did this?' rasped Samuel Sniper. 'Whoever it was, he'll have to pay for it. Have you got him locked up tight?'

'Nope,' Casey said.

'Well, you'd better see to it.'

'No longer my responsibility.'

The chairman took a step towards him. 'What the hell d'you mean by that?'

Casey reached into his pocket and laid his silver badge on the table in front of the group. 'I've quit, as of now.'

'You can't do that!'

'I'm doing it.'

As the men stood silent Casey continued. 'I'm gettin' tired of trying to keep men from killing theirselves. I've decided I'm gonna marry a good woman an' become a sodbuster, get my hands dirty.'

'But you're leaving the town without a law officer. There'll be no control. Anything can happen. The citizens won't be safe.'

Casey smiled. How easily scared were these gentlemen.

'If you and the council will take my advice, even if you haven't asked for it, I suggest that you appoint my deputy, Jesse France, to take over without delay. He's keen, honest an' will be better in the job than I ever was.

'And,' Casey continued, speaking slowly, 'I further advise that you give up any idea of allowing Walt Grayson or anybody else to run this town. He's tough, but I reckon it might be some time before he can return to his ranch. His influence is over. It's up to you to make it stick.'

He turned and strode to the door, leaving the council members gazing at each other. 'I'll pick up my back pay tomorrow.' He left without waiting for a response.

His steps were light. A new career at his age was exciting, as was the thought of marrying Sarah. He knew he had much to learn, but he was ready for that. And so, it seemed, was Sarah.

Moreover, at Buck's suggestion, they had persuaded Molly and her boyfriend from the Double Bar T, to come and work for them. This, Sarah had explained, would release her from domestic chores to spend more time instructing her new husband.

20

After Buck had left for town Moose had been kept busy attending to the rancher, who was in a bad way and who had been calling angrily for water and fresh bandages. He stowed the bodies of the dead men in one of the sheds and covered them with a tarp.

The undertaker was the first to arrive and he carried the bodies away without stopping for coffee.

'Sorry, Sam,' he said. 'Keep it for me when I have more time.'

The doc came shortly afterwards and soon had dressings on Sam's leg and the rancher's hip.

'You were lucky,' he told Sam. 'Walt's gonna be laid up for quite a while, though. The bullet went right through. Probably hit a bone. I've done all I can for now so it's best if he rests the night here. Moose can bring him in tomorrow and I'll see what damage has been done. I've given him something for the pain. He'll maybe seem a mite confused.'

He stayed briefly for coffee, but he, too, had urgent business back in town.

'Thanks, Doc,' Sam said, and watched as he rode away.

After that Sam had remained silent and it was she who first heard the sound of approaching riders.

'Moose,' she called quietly. 'Hand me my gun and see who's out there.'

Moose left the rancher, passed over Sam's Colt and peered out of the window. He turned away quickly and snatched up his own gun.

'Two men,' he whispered. 'One hard looking, the other a younger man, only a kid.'

'Hello the house!' The call was made by the younger man. 'You got Pa in there?'

Moose went to open the door.

'Careful, Moose,' Sam said and pushed herself up from the bed. She checked her gun and held it ready.

Moose opened the door and stood on

the step with the Colt in plain sight. He had already recognized Wilf, the youngest of the rancher's sons.

'You're not welcome here,' he said.

'Who've ya got in there?' Wilf demanded.

'Miss Merryman and me.'

No sooner had he spoken than Walt Grayson's voice, weak though it was, could be heard.

'That you, Wilf?'

Wilf scowled. 'Yeah, Pa, it's me.'

Before Moose had time to whip his gun into position the gunman, still sitting his horse, had brought his Colt up.

'Do ya wanna die?' he snarled. 'Now drop it!'

Moose did.

'Keep him in yer sights,' Wilf said. 'We're goin' in.' He slid from the saddle, drew his own gun and strode towards the door. When he saw his pa lying down with blood-soaked bandages he rushed forward, ignoring Sam who was holding her Colt ready.

'Who did this to you?'

The rancher pointed at Moose. 'Dang well shot me when I wasn't even pointing my gun at him.'

Wilf swung round. 'I'm gonna kill ya fer that. Step outside.'

Moose shrugged. 'I've shucked my gun.'

Wilf drew his lips back in a snarl. 'That won't make no difference. Yer gonna die whether ya've got a gun in yer hand or not.'

He spoke to the gunman who was closely watching everyone in the room. 'You stay here. Keep an eye on her while I do what I gotta do.'

Sam, who had already laid her own gun down, said, 'No more killing!'

'He has to pay for what he's done.' Wilf, who was possibly acting big in front of his pa, gestured at Moose. 'Get outside!'

Walt raised his hand. 'Moose was responsible for murdering your two brothers. It makes no difference who pulled the trigger, and you're right, he must pay. But that's my responsibility. I must avenge the deaths of my sons. Help me up.'

'No!' Sam screamed.

'It's a man's rights,' Walt said. 'A woman won't understand that.'

Wilf, after a brief hesitation, put his hands under his pa's arms and hoisted him to his feet. Walt groaned.

'You can't do it, Pa. Let me.'

Walt rounded on his son. 'I've told you. Get me outside. Then bring that sonofabitch out and strap a gun on him. I won't shoot an unarmed man.'

Sam limped forward. 'Please, Walt. I've always respected you even if I haven't agreed with you. Don't do this. Let the law deal with it. If you don't it'll be you who are guilty of murder.'

Walt faced her. 'It's something I have to do, Sam. Even if you don't see that now you will later.' He continued his painful shuffle to the door, leaning heavily on his son for support.

But Sam wasn't finished. 'Walt, you asked me to marry you and I will, but you've got to give up this idea of revenge.'

Walt stopped. 'You made yourself clear earlier, Sam.'

'I know, Walt, and I'm not saying I didn't mean what I told you then. But we could make a go of it with good will on both sides.'

'Don't trust her, Pa!' Wilf shouted. 'She's bin sheltering those two killers.'

Walt's head twisted round. 'Shut up, Wilf! Let me think.' For a moment he closed his eyes against the pain in his hip and the confusion in his mind. When he opened them again he said, 'Sorry, Sam. We'll talk about that when I'm done here.'

Once outside the rancher was able to stand by himself. 'Go and fetch Moose. Then give him a gun.'

'Are ya sure you wanna do this, Pa?'

'Do as I say!'

Wilf brought Moose out and gave him a gunbelt to strap on. He carefully handed him a Colt.

'Holster it. One wrong move an' I won't hesitate. There's one slug in the chamber, but ya won't have time to use it,' he sneered.

Moose wondered whether he would

even be given the opportunity to draw the gun. If the rancher wasn't fast enough to beat him to the draw he was certain he would be shot by Walt's son. He noted that the .45 in Wilf's hand was pointing steadily at him.

He stood ready.

Buck had thought of his brother as he rode out of town, trying to analyse his own feelings. He loved his brother. Still did. Outlaw or not, Ray could rely on Buck to support and protect him, if it came to that.

He approached Sam's homestead in a relaxed state of mind, contemplating the possibility of meeting up with Ray again after such a long time.

He reined in at the top of the rise.

What he saw caused him to catch his breath and urge his mount forward.

He raced down the slope. As he approached the yard he yelled, 'Lower your weapons! I'm coming in!'

This had little effect except to cause the men to turn their heads at this unexpected sound, even Wilf, who briefly took his attention from Moose. Buck reined in as he reached the yard, and before his horse had stopped he leapt from the saddle.

'What's going on?'

Walt glared. 'Keep out of this.' He turned back to Moose. 'Draw, you sonofabitch!'

Moose had seized the opportunity presented to him by Buck's sudden arrival and had already drawn. Praying that there was really a round in the chamber he yelled at Wilf:

'Lower your gun!'

Wilf did no such thing and Moose pulled the trigger.

Nothing happened except a dull click.

Wilf grinned and fired back. But Moose had moved and the slug parted his hair.

Buck's Colt cracked and Wilf staggered. Slowly he sank to the ground, his gun slipping from his hand. Moose, seeing Walt Grayson turning in his direction flung himself down, rolled and made a grab for Wilf's weapon. He pointed it at the rancher.

'Don't make me shoot,' he said. 'Let the gun go. It's all over.' He sprang to his feet.

Walt Grayson swayed where he stood, staring down at his son, who lay in a pool of blood. He looked around as if he couldn't believe what had happened. His shoulders slumped. His gun arm hung loose. His eyes glazed.

Moose went over to him and took the gun, picked him up gently and carried him towards the house.

'What the hell's been going on?' Buck demanded.

'You arrived just in time,' Moose told him. 'I reckoned my last moment had come.'

'Happy to return the favour,' Buck said.

He was relieved when Sam appeared in the doorway and signalled that she was all right. He bent over the body of Wilf, the third and last son of the rancher, and confirmed that he was dead.

He straightened up as a gunshot came from the house. He raced across, realizing that his first thoughts were for Sam. He found her, staring down in shock at the body of the gunman. Walt Grayson was standing over him, a gun in his hand.

As Buck watched, the rancher crumpled, sank to the ground and lay there. Moose picked him up and took him into the other room.

Buck looked at Sam for an explanation.

'I'm not sure why Walt did it,' she said. 'I think he imagined I was being threatened and he wanted to protect me. And that was when he … it happened so quickly.'

Buck knelt and examined the man. 'Who is he?'

'I've never seen him before,' Sam said. 'And I don't reckon he meant me any harm.'

There was silence except for the rasping breaths of the gunman. Then they stopped and he lay still in death.

It was over.

Buck stood and looked into Sam's eyes.

In those eyes he saw his own future.

Their eyes locked and he held her gaze for a long moment.

'I have to search for my brother,' he said softly.

Sam nodded.

Buck breathed hard. 'But I can't lose you.'

She nodded again. ✦